The Night of One Hundred Thieves

a novel by
DEVON TREVARROW FLAHERTY

Owl and Zebra Press
Durham   Detroit

Owl and Zebra Press
PO Box 62412 Durham NC 27715
owlandzebrapress@gmail.com
Visit our website at owlandzebrapress.wordpress.com

First paperback edition, March 2015
ISBN 978-0-9889651-3-3
E-book available, ISBN 978-0-9889651-4-0
and 978-0-9889651-5-7

Cover art copyright © 2015 by Devon Trevarrow Flaherty
Author photograph copyright © 2013 by Kevin Danforth Flaherty
Illustrations copyright © 2015 by Devon Trevarrow Flaherty
Cover design by Owl and Zebra Press
Deadly Breakfast font by Mark Larsson and used by permission

This book is a work of fiction. Names, characters, places and incidents are either products of the author's imagination or used fictitiously. Any resemblance to actual events or persons, living or dead, is entirely accidental.

Design by Owl and Zebra Press

Printed in the United States of America

✿

for the people who wanted to know more about The Queen,
the ring, and Northwyth

Other Storykeeper Tales by Flaherty:

Benevolent

CONTENTS

The Night of
One Hundred Thieves

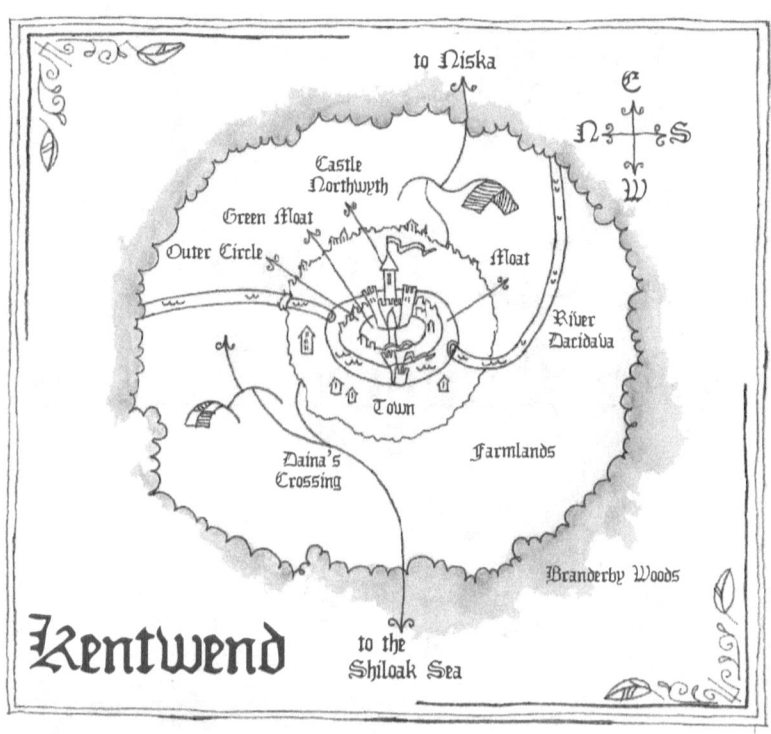

to Niska

Castle
Northwyth

Green Moat

Outer Circle

Moat

River
Daridava

Town

Farmlands

Daina's
Crossing

Branderby Woods

Kentwend

to the
Shiloak Sea

THE CHARACTERS

THE THIEVES

Agnes the Chambermaid – Agnes is The Queen's chief chambermaid. She becomes Lulu's chambermaid when The Queen dies.

Aren, Farrah's Lackey – Aren is a jack-of-all-trades, general thug, and petty criminal for Farrah the Barren.

Berenice the Healer – Berenice appears in the legend version of the Northwyth stories found in *Benevolent*. He is a principal Kentwend healer and potion master and the cousin and confidant of Daina the Drunk's Wife.

Blaise the Traveler – Blaise is the unofficial leader of the Travelers making their way to Kentwend, Northwyth for the royal grave robbing.

Bricteva – Bricteva is the sister Triplet. She is a street performer, singer, and dancer.

Brom – Brom is one of the brother Triplets. He is a street performer and contortionist.

Butrus – Butrus is one of the brother Triplets. He is a street performer and magician.

Daina the Drunk's Wife – Daina is Cecily's neighbor and Berenice's cousin. She was once much closer with Berenice and still uses her ample talent at potion-making to cover Berenice's failings.

Drakon the Traveler – Drakon is one of the Travelers making their way to Kentwend, Northwyth for the royal grave robbing.

Farrah the Barren – Farrah is an Outer Circle widow of a courtier. She now runs a racket in the black market, illegal trades, and high-class robberies with the help of her lackey, Aren.

Herman the Soldier – Herman is Stephyn's brother, an accomplished soldier in the King's army, and usually on castle duty. He is a family man with slim means to support an extended family.

Hero the Player – Hero is one of a group of play actors in Kentwend.

Hilary the Concubine – Hilary appears in the legend version of the Northwyth stories found in *Benevolent*. She is a new addition to the Old Harem and despises her life as a concubine. She makes unlikely friends with Lykus the Cupbearer after the death of her only friend, Meng.

Irene the Courtier – Irene is Maram's best friend and daughter of the Third Courtier. Her and her family's future is grim, thanks to the machinations of Farrah the Barren.

Kori the Farmer – Kori is one of the Band of Farmers and a friend of Rufus the Baker.

Kyros the Advisor – Kyros is one of the advisors to King Jaden. He has been waiting for a promotion in housing and status for a long time and eventually turns to Farrah the Barren for help.

Laurent the Farmer – Laurent is one of the Band of Farmers. He acts as their spokesperson, as a small but articulate member.

Linos the Farmer – Linos is one of the Band of Farmers.

Lykus the Cupbearer – Lykus appears in the legend version of the Northwyth stories found in *Benevolent*. He is older and more careful than his new friend Hilary the Concubine, but is willing to risk everything for friendship and the promise of youth.

Manno the Farmer – Manno is one of the Band of Farmers. He is a real brute in size, used to intimidate opponents of the Farmers.

Maram the Courtier – Maram is a courtier of the Outer Circle and Irene's best friend and supporter through the Third Courtier's demise.

Musa the Traveler – Musa is the only woman in the group of Travelers making their way to Kentwend, Northwyth for the royal grave robbing. She is admired by Seti, soothing to Raban, and abused by Blaise.

Nikeas – Nikeas is the youngest, unmarried son of The Queen and King Jaden. He wants desperately to inherit the throne and is fed up with his station as the youngest son. His only true friend is his youngest sister, Teva.

Nora the Girl Widow – Nora is a peasant, widowed as a teenager during her honeymoon. She is blackmailed by Farrah the Barren and Aren, Farrah's Lackey, for patronage and favors.

Otho the Farmer – Otho is one of the Band of Farmers. He is a real brute in size, used to intimidate opponents of the Farmers.

Panther the Pickpocket – Panther built his career on following the crowds entertained by the freakish Triplets. He moves in their circles as their closest friend and ally.

Raban the Traveler – Raban is one of the Travelers making their way to Kentwend, Northwyth for the royal grave robbing. Raban is hulking and remedial, protected by his cousin, Seti, and tender toward Musa, the only woman in the group.

Rufus the Baker – Rufus is Cecily's stepson. He is sulky and dim but family-oriented and capable of compassion.

Seti the Traveler – Seti is one of the Travelers making their way to Kentwend, Northwyth for the royal grave robbing. He is Raban's cousin and protector and Blaise's greatest challenge.

Stephyn the Old Acolyte – Stephyn is one of the helpers of the Head Saint, too old for his station. He is being shifted into his brother Herman's household, against both of their wishes.

Tarquis the Secret Pirate – His real name is Tarquis, but at the time of the legend, he was known in Kentwend as Merek. Tarquis is a traveler through Kentwend, a pirate hiding out as he changes lives across a continent.

Theobald the Taverno – Theobald owns the Tavern where the thieves converge to make their plans. He is also the royally appointed provider of the soldiers' evening mess and mead.

THOSE WHO WERE NOT THIEVES

The Angel – The Angel is an original character from the Northwyth legends as told in *Benevolent*. The Angel was once involved with The Queen but was separated from her by his immortality and purpose. He may have fathered a secret love child.

Brando the Heir – Brando is the oldest son of The Queen and King Jaden and therefore the heir of the throne of Northwyth. He lives in the castle with his family and the next in line, his son Felix.

Cecily the Baker's Widow – Cecily is the Widow of the former Baker and stepmother to his grown children, including Rufus. She still believes in magic, despite herself, and is shyly in love with her close friend, Conover the Storykeeper.

Conover the Storykeeper – Conover is Kentwend's official and royal Storykeeper. A peasant who is secretly in love with Cecily the Baker's Widow, he has been asked to sire a successor to his position.

Dion the Oracle – Like the Farmers' Almanac of ancient times, Dion foretells weather, births, deaths, couplings, social affairs, strange occurrences, and royal movements, among other things. He is friends with Conover and Cecily, a force to be both admired and feared.

Fedel the Heir's Wife – Fedel is the wife of Brando, the heir to the throne of Northwyth.

Felix the Next Heir – Felix is a teenage prince, a grandson of The Queen and King Jaden, and son of Brando and Fedel. He is the second in ascendancy to the throne of Northwyth.

The Head Saint – The Head Saint is the chief holy man of Kentwend, where he performs religious rites, attends the dying, and leads ceremonies, among other things.

Ingrid the Tutor – Ingrid is Princess Lulu's chaperone and tutor. The two have only recently arrived in Kentwend to further Lulu's education in ladyship.

Jaden the King – Also known as **Jaden the Great** in the original Northwyth legends. He came to his kingship through marriage to The Queen, when he was just a brave and talented soldier.

Lulu the Princess – Lulu is a princess and granddaughter of The Queen and King Jaden. She now lives at the Castle with Ingrid, her chaperone and tutor, in order to receive a lady's education.

Osmund – Osmund is a child, a prince, and the second son of Brando, the heir to the throne.

The Queen – The Queen of Northwyth is a figure in the original Northwyth legends and the central figure of most of the stories. She is legendarily brave, wise, steady, and beautiful, and some of the stories portray her as larger than life or even magical.

The Sage – An original character to the Northwyth legends, The Sage has longevity, as well as telepathic powers and great wisdom. He is allied to The Queen.

Teva – Teva is a princess, the youngest, unmarried daughter of The Queen and King Jaden. She lives in the castle, resembles her mother, and is fiercely loyal to Nikeas despite his jealousy.

ffoecevoord

Some call it the night of thieves, and others call it the night of one hundred thieves. There were not one hundred thieves, as you shall soon see. There were exactly thirty-two thieves. But to call it the night of thirty-two thieves would be to suck the magic from the thing, and magic is what the night was all about.

The point is, there were many thieves; many more than is usual—or useful—for thievery. There was one ring to steal. The Queen's Alchemist and Jeweler had made the ring from interwoven, rare, and beautiful metals, chips of many precious gems, and one giant, ruby-colored stone. The stone was of unsurpassed beauty and contained one-half of an extremely powerful magic seed. Thirty-two thieves. One ring. Ah, now we see where the story becomes interesting.

This story is a legend. When told, it is usually done in a quick session around a campfire or as an addendum to either the great long drama of The Queen's life and times or the weaving history of the ring itself. This time, the whole mess will get our attention. Remember: thirty-two thieves, one ring.

But perhaps we should lay out the history, too, just in case you are unfamiliar.

The magic seed pre-existed The Queen. Its earliest known history is with the Mysterious Hag. From there, The Angel found it and delivered it to The Queen—although some versions say that she went to The Angel only for advice about the seed. The Queen—a powerful, benevolent, and wise ruler and an only, unmarried child—left her kingdom in the thick of the War to the Death against The Dark One and the Demonis. She journeyed to find and unlock an unnamed power that would save the kingdom of Northwyth. She met The Angel in the middle of a vast desert when she was exhausted almost to death, and they fell immediately and irrevocably in love in the moments between her arrival, their brief telekinetic conversation, the handing over of the seed in a leather pouch, and a crash of sand and heat that consumed The Angel into vanishing.

During the final battle of the War to the Death, The Dark One struck The Queen, slicing through the ivory flesh of her arm but not before slicing through the pouch and the tiny seed. The seed was severed in half and released a behemoth blast of power that—in great confusion and a reckless disregard for the laws of physics—defeated the Demonis, killed The Dark One, and ended the war.

One half of the seed was later enclosed in a golden locket. The locket was engraved with an "A" and sealed with a lock that had no key. It disappeared. The other half of the seed The Queen gave to her alchemist. He magically encased the half-seed in a red gem. Then The Queen gave the gem to her Jeweler, who placed it in a setting of astonishing brilliance: the ring. The Queen wore the ring for her long lifetime and was buried with it.

The legend does not end there, and the Northwyth story doesn't even begin there. But for our purposes, that is what happened, plus or minus human flight, a dragon, an eerie magician, and some mind-reading. The locket will surface; the storykeepers will keep on collecting and telling stories; the destinies of nations and the fates of a woodsboy, a maid, a midwife, a dog, a set of space-age siblings, a punk rocker, and an academic will hang in the balance; and the Shadow will make off with the ring.

Who is the Shadow? Now, telling here wouldn't be half as much fun.

Twenty Years Before

Deep ruts crested at the side of the road, hardening into long ridges, stony underneath but slick on the top. A drizzle had persisted until afternoon, when the sky broke open to the blue beyond, washing a glistening world in golden sunlight.

Cecily stood in the mud. She shuffled her leather clogs without noticing she was doing so. Her long dress hung spattered and stained with old offenses at the bottom. In the crowd, she hugged her grocery basket tightly to her breast. Cecily strained her head out on her neck. Was it coming? Would she be able to see? Was it possible the sky always turned blue and reflected heaven ahead of The Queen?

Tales of The Queen flourished in the streets of Northwyth. Old wives tittered them up and down the alleyways. The puppet shows were peppered with spectacularly ugly Demonis and told grandiose tales of The Queen, of King Jaden, and of a time before peace, even back to the times of The Sage. Mothers leaned over beds in flickering lamplight to whisper to their children, shadows cast up from their chins, about The Angel, hinting at the affair and the missing love child.

But Cecily could no longer allow herself to believe those tales, because you outgrew those things, didn't you? If she believed, the other girls would laugh at her. No man would want her. She would become part of a story herself, part of the gossip like Berenice the Healer, the odd Triplets, Conwen the Storykeeper, and the others who were spoken of with pity. The profound touch of magic could live among you, but only if reduced to nothing more than words and laughter.

It is a right of passage for each generation, perhaps: to deny the legends of the fathers, failing to notice that magic is still happening all around. There is a time of slumber between every bright day. There is, indeed, nothing new under the sun, or deep in the night, or even woven, nearly lost, in our sleep.

Cecily let her mind wander from stories to her dreams of a well-built man, a warm house, and a couple of clean-faced children. Then the crowd around her grew louder and more agitated. She was forced to clutch the grocery basket tighter as pedestrians jostled her from all sides. Someone called out, "What is it?" And someone else, "It's The Queen!"

All eyes scanned the road to the west—where it crested a hill and then was absorbed in the Branderby Woods. The hill was gradual, cheerful, and rounded, flashing grasses on its shoulders before the wooly darkness of woods. The road stretched up, a ribbon of salmony brown. Cecily noticed movement at the hill's apex: a rhythmic bobbing twinkle of reflected light. Almost imperceptibly it grew bigger and higher. The reflection shone from the top of a staff, glinting silver in the sun. The flag rose slowly, followed by the standard of the House of Northwyth. Then, quickly, up from the top of the hill other glints, other shapes and colors multplied, and soon there mounted a procession of horses and riders, attendants, and an open carriage adorned with brilliant fabrics that floated listlessly on the breeze.

The sound of the procession had not yet reached the villagers, who crowded into the flatland to watch. Some of the children broke free from the crowd and ran up the gentle slope along the road to meet the train. Other townspeople were already joining the procession and paraded from the forest clinging to its sides and straggling behind.

Cecily heard a horn piercing through the shouts. Its song rose intermittently on the shifting breezes. It did not play a melody but blasts meant to call attention to the procession, to announce its coming. The crowd around Cecily quieted, and she could also hear the brusque chanting of the soldiers marching fore and aft of the carriage. What they chanted, Cecily could not discern. Something to keep them uniform, to keep the pace, which sounded like "Up! Pah! Oh! Ah!" and "Up! Pah! Oh! Ah!"

In a mob, the crowd lurched first one way and then the other, and Cecily moved to her tip-toes in welcome excitement. She was a tall girl, anyhow, but was not yet fully grown. Her auburn hair she wore up loosely on her head and hid it under a lace-trimmed cap, except where a few wavy locks had worked free. They tickled at her neck and chin and grazed her white shoulders. Her skin was white, pale, smudged with dirt and soot, and callused only on the hands and feet. She was slim and shapely, her loosely fitted dress and wrap-around apron somehow making her feel naked in her new body. She averted her almond, brown eyes whenever she encountered men.

But now, her eyes were fixed on the road from the far hill, watching the spectacular show descend into the farmland and approach her. It was a sight. And the front horse and horseman were almost there! Was someone riding Son of Quicklander in the procession?

The soldiers grew close enough that Cecily could hear a horse snort in a rattling gust. She suddenly remembered that she had picked flowers and placed them on top of her groceries. She looked down, frowned at a few cracked eggs, and snatched up the flowers. She worked her arm out in the jostling crowd, found a moment when the way parted before her, and flung the flowers into the road just before the wheels of the carriage churned over them.

Cecily yelled, "Life and prosperity to The Queen!" and saw The Queen. The Queen's carriage was open, meant for tours such as this when The Queen wanted to be seen and to see her kingdom. It was gold and white on the outside, lined inside with midnight-blue velvet, and The Queen sat alone atop it. She waved to her people, slow and practiced. The Queen commanded awe. She was tall and handsome, with long red hair that shone coppery in the sunlight. Her skin flashed clean and beautified. She was indisputably strong and imposing, meant for warfare as much as any banquet room. Her red lips parted over the whitest of teeth; her green eyes looked steadily at all the uproar as she swayed gently, high over the road.

Cecily could not help herself. The Queen's presence was heavy, like storm rain, and was searing, like a cattle brand. Cecily *did* believe the stories, every one of them. She was a child again, was telling herself she would always be a child in her heart because the stories were real, were instructive, enjoyable, important. Would she have to hide her belief away, then? In the presence of The Queen she could have yelled it out. But then, when she went back into town tomorrow to barter, what would people think? Would she become Cecily the Woman-Child? Cecily the Soft Head? Unworthy of progeny, unworthy of love? Perhaps she could seek the protection of the Head Saint, live chaste as a servant to the apothecaries. But as soon as the complicated thoughts arose, they blew away again with the pomp and excitement happening all around her, and Cecily lifted an arm to hail The Queen.

As The Queen turned her face to the opposite side of the road, her hand also moved in that direction, and a beam of sunlight caught one of her adornments. The light refracted a ruby-colored gleam, and it caught the crowd unawares, caught Cecily right in the eye. She could not look away and followed the beam back to its source: an enormous, red stone fixed in an intricate ring on The Queen's elegant hand.

It was not like the little reflections one saw on a sunny day everywhere around town, on the small crests of the river water, and off the tin-maker's cart. Cecily had seen with her own eyes that the ring had shot out a ray of red light amplified in brightness and intensity. It had transfixed her, had mesmerized her, had magicked her, and they—the elect standing on the right side of Gretl's Way— had all seen it, had all felt it, like an arrow to the chest.

¤

Farrah massaged her forehead with her fingertips and rubbed towards her hair line. Her head ached. She looked across the room and out of the pane of rippled glass beside the front door at a world of distorted passersby and diffused, grayed sun. Every note that twanged from the zither made her wince, especially the discordant ones.

Irene, her back to Farrah, was unaware of Farrah's distraction, unaware of Farrah wincing and rubbing at her temples. The child's eyes were narrowed at the zither, her tongue working its way out of her lips as she wrestled with her fingers, the strings, and the song she had just been taught.

"Alright, child!" Farrah brought her hand down to her side with a snap and heaved a blasé sigh. Irene stopped immediately and wriggled her posture straighter. "And pull that tongue in. We do not see ladies' tongues unless we are being abused by them."

It was an old saying. But for the most part, Irene had never "seen" Farrah's tongue. Farrah was typically a composed, tall, and willowy woman with heaps of wavy brown hair, russet cheeks, and ruby red lips, carefully magnified by gowns in cranberry velvet or with accents of cranberry in silk ribbons or embroidery. She was generally cheerful, seeming not to notice that she was already getting the moniker Farrah the Barren around town. It had once been Farrah the Fair.

The two lingered in silence for a few minutes. Neither moved, like subjects in an antiquated painting of an affluent society in a bright, stony room, until Farrah said, "You can be quiet; that is a great credit to you, Irene."

"Thank you, m'lady."

"We are done for today. I have things to attend to. You may sit on the step until someone has come to get you. Or is your home close by?"

"I will wait. They say The Queen is passing today. I love to see The Queen." Irene had still not moved from her rigid position seated on the stool on a hemp rug in the middle of the room. Farrah still stood behind her, still looked out the window, but now with a hand resting nonchalantly on Irene's shoulder.

"What do you love about The Queen, Irene?" Farrah was curious but not strongly so.

"The stories, I suppose. I like to think of the magic coming off of her, as she passes, emanating like the heat of the sun and sinking into my skin. I look at her copper hair, her ruby ring, all the things that are part of her story."

"The ring? It is always so interesting to people."

"It encases the seed and powerful magic!" Irene spoke with reverence and awe in hushed tones.

"Well, I suppose so. Or is it just a very beautiful ring, very *desirable*?" At this, Farrah clasped her hands together over her heart and strode slowly to the window, still watching the shapes and colors passing.

Irene leaned forward over her knees, her back straight, and she said in a proud tone, "Our family has a desirable ring, *with* a slave bracelet. It was a queen's once, too. Our family has royal blood, you know. That slave bracelet is our inheritance, the pride of our family, a symbol of our blood," she repeated from rote.

"Is it now? A special slave bracelet? Made all of gold and emeralds, no doubt?" Farrah turned from the window and smiled back at Irene, a bit playful. She wasn't even aware of who Irene's family *was*. The courtiers and other Outer Circle families just sent their children to her with their nannies, maids, or a chaperone and something to barter: a basket of sweet cakes, a pretty piece of silk, or a sachet of spices. It was her honor to pass her skill—both musical and in things less definable—on to young ladies.

Irene looked offended at her teacher. "Better than emeralds! We'd never sell it, so we keep it hidden away. I've even seen it, once. And my grandmother wore it on her wedding day!"

"But is it magical?"

Irene sniffed and raised her chin. "No, it is not."

One Afternoon As Winter Approaches: Twenty Years Later

Ŷrene grew up. Farrah grew cold and hard. Cecily had a rough string of goldenless years.

The Queen became old. She still stood tall and imposing from a life of perfect posture and an education in grace and poise, but her copper hair was now a cascade of gray with a sheen of silver. The ruby ring and its filigreed setting of many-colored metals—silver and gold and bronze and copper and black and white—weighed heavy on her hand. She had headaches, body aches, and fatigue.

King Jaden had aged as well, but at fourteen years The Queen's junior, he had more vim and longevity left him. The kingdom was at peace. The royal ascension was firmly established. No rumors of intrigue festered, just a quiet sadness that The Indelible Queen would not make it through the winter. Dion, the town Oracle, said the winter would be harsh, long, and snowy.

Rufus stood in the dark of a wooden room without windows at midday and whacked at a lump of dough on a slab table, with the butt of his hand—Whomp! Whomp! He whacked all the more severely in rebellion against the throbbing in his shoulder. He was too young for throbbings in his shoulder. How would he pound dough, knead dough, shape dough, and trade baked loaves to the western townspeople if his shoulder seized up? More importantly, who would feed his wife and his children? Or himself? He raised his arm higher, brought it down with a reverberating thud.

As he did so, the door to the bakery clattered open, the pockmarked bell tied to the handle, clunking. Cecily slid in sideways and shut the door behind her. While turning around to him, she said, "You won't get anything good out of that dough, now."

Rufus grunted without looking up, "I'll make brosh."

"People will need brosh this winter." She floated across the room to the counter, still pretty and lithe, although hardened against the edges of the past twenty years, the twenty years since she was fifteen and standing at the roadside to watch The Queen pass. "They say it's going to be…"

"I know what they say. They always have *something* to say. Even if it is a load of dung."

"Well, that may be true. But the Oracle…"

"Is that what you've come here for?" He stopped kneading to look up at her. "To gossip about Dion? Or to beg bread?"

Cecily winced. She was not a gossip. More importantly, she was Rufus's widowed step-mother, had raised him from a child, and was subject to his injustices as the eldest male of their fractured family. He often refused to properly care for his widowed stepmother and for his nieces and nephews, and sometimes would not even throw them the crust of the burnt bread that he fed to his pigs and dogs.

His father had been much less caring. Perhaps Cecily's mothering had given him something after all, then: she had rubbed his poison into mere hardness.

"Yes, of course, to buy bread. Why else would I come here?" She set her basket on the far edge of the slab table and pulled back on the cloth covering. She considered its contents. In a moment, Rufus was shadowing over her from the opposite side of the table. "I don't need eggs," he grumbled. "At least not those tiny, poor ones. You have any metal?"

Her eyes met his, so close to her she was suddenly in an cloud of his warm breath, which smelled of hops and decay. It made her remember sitting on the childrens' bed when they were little, telling them the Northwythan stories. Back then, their breath smelled like sweet cream. It had been torturous work, being punished by their childish hearts because she wasn't the Baker's *first* wife.

Cecily's look at Rufus now was more inquisitive. Deep hurts and fears mingled with her obstinacy. He stared her down, but in his eyes she saw what others didn't: an imprisoned compassion, a moody young man apprenticing in his father's shadow, transformed into a scarred family man, attacking the world as it had attacked him.

"I never have metal," she said.

"Well, I need metal."

"What would you need metal for?"

This time, he just glowered at her.

"How about this wool? It's a nice piece. Big enough for a dress for Mirian. And enough to keep me in bread for a couple weeks, eh?"

Rufus sighed, heaving the sound up through his sizable torso and extra-broad shoulders, and throwing it out at the room. A gust of wind rattled at the door, then silenced. Rufus sidled back over to the dough. He reached into a barrel at his side and drew flour into his fist, sprinkled it on the mound, and continued kneading.

"Rufus?"

"What? You still here?"

Cecily gathered herself, straightened up. "You know I am still here. I have made a business proposition. With what you offer me, I could go to the baker across town. But we are family."

"Family. Humph. That just means more beggars."

Cecily began packing her things. "I am *not* a beggar. I offer you goods." She stopped suddenly, looked up at him. "Although, *if* you were to follow the traditions of our people, you would know that I could never *be* a beggar to you. I am your widowed mother!" Her eyes flamed up with life.

"My *step*mother," Rufus said, carefully and with an acidic twist of pity.

"Again, *if* you had a sense of tradition, you would realize they are one and the same." Rufus stopped kneading and looked up to her, standing red-cheeked with fury, her basket and cloak gathered about her. She always looked handsomer and stronger when she was worked up. It had been a dangerous quality to have as the Baker's Wife.

"Calm down, *Mother*. Choose some bread. Leave the wool." He lowered his gaze back to the dough as he picked up a flat tool, portioned out the dough, and rolled each portion into a ball. Cecily watched him for a while, calming her pride so that she could walk over to the wall of wooden cubbies and baskets and take some bread. She chose a large oval loaf, tapered at both ends and sprinkled with teensy, red seeds. Then she placed the wool on the far end of the table, where Rufus kept his ledger and an ink pot with a quill propped inside.

"Good day, Rufus," she said over her shoulder.

Cecily already had the door open when Rufus started to speak, and she paused a moment to listen. "You better hope your *magic* is real. Without it, you have nothing."

She slipped out.

◻

Conover looped the red ribbon around his outside door pull, then tied it, letting the ends fall, flitting in the breeze. That breeze harbored a real nip, something ominous hidden inside. It was barely harvest time, and already winter was crouched at the edge of the woods.

Conover looked one last time down the narrow, dirt road. The road fell in wide steps between the parallel walls of wooden buildings, shop signs, and clothes flailing from upstairs windows, to where it turned to the left and disappeared. Cecily still wasn't coming. Well, he had to go, but the ribbon would suffice. Cecily knew what the ribbon meant. Red for the castle, purple for bartering, emerald for church, amber for work, white for her house, brown for visiting.

"Sir! It is time to go." The royal messenger stood at an angle beside Conover's door, erect and impassive.

"Yes, alright." Conover turned uphill and motioned for the messenger to lead away. He followed.

They wound through Kentwend, mostly over packed dirt roads between tightly built houses and shops, up a few alleyways bricked down the middle for drainage, and eventually to the more central part of town. Approaching the Main Bridge, the streets widened and shone with golden-hued stones, lined by buildings of an airier sort: railed balconies, broad stairways up to front doors, colored standards and family crests snapping in the chill wind, glass windows merrily winking back at the sun and distorting the white-capped women standing behind them, looking out as if they were women drowning without a fight.

As they approached the castle, it loomed higher and blocked out more of the sun so that the light seemed trapped at its shoulders, stuck to its various arches and turrets and irregular outcroppings high above. The life at its base grew muted and felt damp, and then cut off at a wide, geometrical, stone-paved moat. The broad thoroughfare Conover and the messenger walked became a bridge, which began and terminated at monstrous guard houses of golden-tan stone. They walked through the first of the checkpoints, the doors thrown open, without impediment. At the second, the messenger paused to give his credentials and they continued deeper into the castle's shadow.

The outer ring of the castle—affectionately called the Outer Circle—was really just more town cradled inside the protection of the moat. It contained a smattering of shops for royal employees and sanctioned wares, and the homes of courtiers, advisors, and other prominent land-owners. Among the buildings stood the homes of the old royal blood. Since the only royal blood that ran through Kentwend, through all of Northwyth and the world, now came directly from The Queen and included only her five children and her fourteen grandchildren, most of the old unneeded homes had been transformed into other things: a meeting hall, a public bath.

Conover and the messenger cut through the Outer Circle on the rising street until it met with the second "moat" of the Castle. The Green Moat by name was really a lawn: a wide, carefully manicured green, as geometric and encircling of The Castle as the first moat. It was lined with stone walls, upon which a man might lean forward and rest his arms. In peace time, and on this day, there were colorfully-clad women and men meandering on the Green Moat, leisurely strolling and wrapping cloaks tighter against the cold without disrupting the effect of their miniature braids, which fell just so across their pinched-rouge cheeks. A high ringing laughter, like a bell, rose to Conover on a breeze as they passed by on the road.

After they crossed over the Green Moat on a bridge, the road opened up into a stone courtyard. The courtyard was surrounded by high walls, around the top of which ran a promenade. Directly ahead rose the castle's Main Gate, a giant entrance in which a six-horse-high, four-man-thick wood door sometimes stood. On this morning, the massive door had been lowered to the ground where it sat in a deep groove in the stone courtyard, and Conover and the messenger stepped up onto it like a stage. At intervals, stairs had been carved into the wood, and it was on these stairs Conover stepped up onto the door and proceeded into the castle proper.

He was somewhat of a regular here. Even though he was a layman and came from a long line of laymen, his meals were supported by the patronage of the castle. It was a very old tradition to keep the Storykeeper safe and comfortable enough so that he might devote much of his time to gathering and telling stories. In return, the Storykeeper not only gathered stories from Kentwend and beyond and told them daily to the children, the parsons, the monks, the playwrights, and to travelers, but he also told them at the castle. He often wandered to the castle and walked the halls and cavernous rooms looking for someone to talk to. Sometimes he was formally invited to entertain the royal subjects and fine-mannered guests during a revel or a visitation.

The messenger led him through the front courtyard and the entrance hall, and into the Great Hall, where The Queen was in state, seated on her oversized, ornate throne. The throne would dwarf anyone, but The Queen appeared to have shrunken since the last time Conover had been here. Her jewels dangled on her fingers and at her wrist. Her thin neck rose bird-like from layers of sumptuous materials, knits, and her quilted robe. Surely she could not have worn the heavy robe from her rooms to this place. She looked far too frail for that. He wondered if it was possible her ample crown was attached to the throne so that her shining, silvery mane could support it?

Her eyes flashed down at Conover, merriment behind what was graying and wrinkling, slowly and surely. "Storykeeper," she began. Conover normally preferred his first name to his title, but when The Queen called him Storykeeper, it was a conferred honor. "Storykeeper, we have entered a new season. In this season, I need to speak of matters of great importance to those who will continue these things *in the next season.*" Her voice still carried weight, and it echoed in the near-empty hall.

"Yes, Your Majesty."

"Among these things, the fate of the Storykeeper is of great importance."

"I am honored, Queen."

"I do not fear for your safety, nor do I believe you will stop doing what it is you do so well and with such great care. Your family has always been careful with your traditions," she sighed and allowed herself a look of affection, "and for that I truly thank you."

"No, thank you." Conover fell to one knee and bowed his head.

"Conover."

He looked up, startled. The Queen had spoken frankly with him many times before as he walked with her around the grounds or entered her private quarters to witness a new heir, but she had never called him his given name from the throne. "What I need from you is an apprentice. I hope that means blood, but I will accept otherwise if blood is not possible."

Conover reddened. He was not young but he was also not too old to sire children. Although he had never spoken of it, he knew whom he wanted to bear him an apprentice. In all the years of adolescence and early manhood, he had silently rejected the prospects before him. He could never love any of Kentwend's rugged, brash peasants. But when Cecily went from the Baker's Wife to the Baker's Widow, his hopes opened like a flower before he could tamp them down. Now, every day, he lived in a constant flux between hope and repression, love and shyness, friendship and fear, that forever resulted in paralysis.

The Queen waited in bemused silence. Conover cleared his throat. "Your Majesty, I will do as you bid."

The Queen suddenly looked older, a hint of anxiety or exhaustion lining her majestic face. "Please, Conover. Marry. If that does not produce an apprentice, then find one. Storykeepers are very rare and precious and we need you to continue our traditions and tell our history. Find an apprentice with haste. I would like to see—"

"You mean…?"

"This winter," it echoed down and back up the room. "Storykeeper, find the next chapter of your own story. May it be a happy one."

◘

Agnes slid a finger down the side of a cut crystal decanter. She removed a rag from a pocket of her work dress and used the cleanest corner to buff the surface to a shine. She set the decanter carefully back on the delicate table that stood at the side of The Queen's bed. It tinked against its matching cup as it came to rest. Agnes let her hand graze over the surface of the metal box that also adorned the table. She eyed the heavy lock, knowing that even if someone should break the best lock that the world could offer, there would be nothing inside to claim. The Queen always wore the ring. Agnes wondered why she even had a lock box for it.

Agnes pushed the rag back into her pocket, where she kept her fingers wrapped around it, leaving her hand bulging in the folds of the castle-standard frock. She sauntered around the large room, looking for things to dust, things to shine, or a fold in the royal bedding to smooth. It was an enormous apartment with ells and ells of stone floor between the giant, curtained four poster, the dressing table, the royal wardrobes, the double doors out to the balcony, and the double doors out to the hallways. At the center of it all, an intricate, colorful hexagonal rug weighed down the center of the room and sat beneath the hexagonal war strategy table.

Almost all the pieces on that table had long ago been moved

to their drawers, where only Agnes ever went to polish them. What was left on the topographic wonder of the kingdom were the figures representing the kings of a few bordering kingdoms, a figure for The Queen, one for King Jaden, and one for The Sage. The ornate Queen stood at the heart of the Kingdom of Northwyth, Jaden in the area of the Woods of Branderby where stag hunting was best, and the wooden Sage afloat in the little crescent of the vast Sea of Shiloak which grazed the edge of the table.

Where was The Sage now? Agnes looked down at the piece and figured she didn't blame people for thinking he was made-up. Children's stories. When he'd last come, she must have been only a girl, just old enough to have been given to the castle as a chambermaid-in-training, eyes large with the wonders of the castle, ears a-prick with the goings on and whispered words that echoed around corners. The kingdom was already enjoying its time of peace, so The Sage would have been on a return visit; for what Agnes had no need to understand. Twenty-five years ago?

She saw him heal Arand with her own eyes, but memories eventually faded. Some memories wore worse than others, when people's wagging tongues got hold of them.

There was no more cleaning she could do here today. She had better air out The Queen's dress for tomorrow, but first she would go fetch water for the basins.

Agnes stepped out into a wide and bright hallway and closed the immensely tall door with a gentle boom. The men's voices were at her back before she had time to turn around. She whirled, set her back against the door, bowed her head, and waited for them to pass. She knew their voices without having to raise her eyes, which she would not have done anyhow. That—the mellow, deep tenor— was the voice of the King, and those were his soft, dark leather riding boots. And that—the whiny, stuttering nasal—was Kyros the Advisor, and those were his rabbit-fur-lined boots.

She studied the patterns in the rug as she waited for the men to progress sufficiently up the hallway, which would take some time at their leisurely pace, as it was full of subconscious fits and starts.

"W-well, really, Your Highness, w-w-we w-will have to address these matters *some*-t-time."

"Could it be? Has it come to this?"

"Dion has said that the w-winter will not pass w-without..."

"Has he, really?" Jaden's irises deepened with profound sadness. "So the Oracle says that she'll die, but what does the doctor say? The other advisors?"

"Sir, I don't know."

"Then I suppose it would be best to have a unity of consensus before we go expecting the worst."

"B-but Dion—and I—and surely you have seen The Queen?"

"Kyros, I am blessed to see The Queen every day I am in Kentwend. I have seen her thousands upon thousands of times. What is it that I am supposed to have missed? Do you mean she has predicted her own death, and I am the only fool?"

"I w-would never call you a fool. I said no such thing." When Jaden stayed silent, lost in rumination, Kyros began again, "I only m-meant to bring up the small m-matter of my moving into the Outer Circle."

"Ah, yes. Your family is still in the village after all this time. You would like to be granted a move before we go into a state of mourning." Jaden's steel blues watched Kyros' startled eyes, his heightened eyebrows. Kyros bit back his words, not risking saying anything more. "Well, despite that you have been so tactless as to lump my wife's eventual death with your housing issues, I can see that you have been overlooked in this area. I will look into it." He lifted his hand to stop Kyros from interrupting or thanking him. "*But* I'm not aware there are any lodgings available at this time. What is your contribution to the crown?"

"B-b-besides my services? My—my land?"

The King just nodded, attempting patience.

"W-well, I am a second son of G-G-Gallan, and our holdings are around one thousand acres, v-very well farmed."

"Not great, is it?"

"B-but, sir…"

"It's all right, Kyros." The King set a heavy hand on Kyros's shoulder, to still him and stop him talking. "We'll have to find a place for you," but The King looked unsure about the prospects, or perhaps just distracted from the issue altogether.

Kyros had his head bent now. He said, "Thank you, Your Highness." And with a whole body salute, a quick flick of rigidness, he turned and walked briskly back the way he had come.

Jaden looked after him, but his thoughts had already shifted inward. Or perhaps it would be better to say his soul's gaze settled somewhere far, far away, in a distant time and perhaps even place. Jaden hadn't been born an heir. The Queen ruled fifteen years alone before she chose her most talented, trusted soldier—a younger flotsam with amazing abilities and a kind heart—to join her on the throne. She had needed a partner with whom to produce an heir or two or three, and since her true love happened to be a fairy-tale angel…

"Grandpa?" Lulu stood in front of him, but it took him a moment to focus in. Then he smiled at his grandchild, a flower among maidens who always elicited a smile from him and most other people she met. She waited until his searching eyes came to rest on her clear, sparkling blue eyes rimmed by a thick line of pale eyelashes under neat, pointed eyebrows. She wore a diadem in her mounds of sandy-blonde curls, and her utterly fashionable tunic dress, although draped, was contoured enough to tell others that she was getting older and very beautiful.

"Lulu!" he said. "I didn't see you." He walked leisurely with her a few yards until they stood on a walkway overlooking one of the banquet rooms—The Queen's room for entertaining, which was open to foot traffic during the day. They looked out over the gleaming stone floors, marble columns, heavy drapes, and gilt sconces. A man crossed the room below, at an angle through the far corner. His blonde hair flashed through a spot of sun.

"Is that a peasant?" Lulu asked.

"That is Conover, the Storykeeper." Jaden lowered his eye to the scene, but not his chin. "You have much to learn, Lulu."

◻

While Lulu was off charming her grandfather, the King, her chaperone and tutor, Ingrid, searched for her. Ingrid said to herself, *She slipped out after breakfast on purpose. She used those delegates as a scrim, the little whippet. And now she's off daydreaming and picking apples while she should be doing her Homer.* Her slippers clicked rhythmically along the corridors. *Lulu may not have a Queen and King to answer to...*

Of course Lulu did have grandmother and grandfather to answer to, but in the same way most children answer to their grandparents, and not as Their Royal Majesties. Lulu had been brought to Kentwend from her father's kingdom to the northwest on the coast of the great, churning Shiloak, when she proved more spirited and distractible than her older siblings. Her mother—a daughter of The Queen and King Jaden—sent her, with her tutor in tow, to learn calm and poise from a change of environment and the strong influence of The Queen.

Quickly Lulu had discovered the castle's system of secret corridors and even more secret corridors. Ingrid, ever the astute tutor, had found them out as well. Ingrid let her mind leaf through her memories, while her body wound through the narrower, more shadowed corridors of the castle. She circled around the main apartments and through the family living spaces. Perhaps she should head toward the workers' quarters or the kitchens or the

Old Harem. Or maybe she ought to head out to the stables and the kitchen gardens. Lulu was more often than not headed through the kitchen gardens out into the castle's back courtyard gard—

As Ingrid came around a curve in a long and narrow stone passageway behind the Royal Dining Hall, she popped out a low, arched doorway and ran headlong into Nikeas, the youngest royal son.

"Ah!" Ingrid screamed. She flailed her arms and hands in overreaction to the collision. The flailing only caused her frocks to become more and more entangled, more and more twisted around her body and up over her head. She continued flailing, now trying to free herself from her spasticity.

"Mind yourself!" yelled a surprised Nikeas as he stepped back out of reach of the cloud of clothing and flailing arms which threatened to overwhelm him as it had overwhelmed Ingrid. His crystalline blue eyes looked miffed, and he watched Ingrid struggle, as he arched an eyebrow at Teva, his sister.

Teva huffed playfully at her brother and then stepped forward to help Ingrid straighten her pointed, veiled hat and smooth over her finery and her composure. "Now, now. There you are. Nikeas is quite sorry that he is such a sour person to encounter around blind corners."

Ingrid looked first at Teva and then over to appraise Nikeas with doubt. "Not at all, not at all. I was really chuffing along there. I was looking for Lulu…"

"Of course you were!" Teva was not much older than Lulu. Aunt and niece were both still under the weight of the royal house, although the elder was of marriageable age. Both had young spirits and quick wits, but Teva was more tempered where Lulu was more temperamental. Teva's eyes danced at the thought of Lulu before they flashed at Nikeas.

"Nikeas? Ahem."

"Yes, um…" He was searching for a name here; even an

appointment would do.

"Ingrid. She is Lulu's chaperone and tutor. You do recall your niece, Lulu, do you not?" More merriment in the eyes. Oh, how Nikeas could be such a bear about anyone outside his small world of siblings and the soldiers whose company he kept. Teva wouldn't put it past him to forget his own niece, but she also knew he would be sore about not appearing gentlemanly in front of her, Teva, his favorite.

Nikeas now turned his irked expression on Teva. "Of course I—!" He then addressed himself to a spot that seemed to be at the base of Ingrid's hat, right at the center of her forehead. "Please forgive me, m'lady. I have not seen Lulu this morning. She has not been in here this past half hour." Then, with a humorless smile at the hat, he bowed slightly and pivoted to his left, where he was standing at a banister that ran the circumference of the large, low, and earthy Arms Room.

On the rectangular, dirt floor frolicked two trainers, one armskeeper, Brando the Heir, and his two healthy sons, Felix and Osmund. Teva, too, turned from Ingrid to link arms with her sister-in-law, Fedel, who was also standing on the promenade, watching the games. Ingrid huffed off, still in search of Lulu, while Teva watched her nephews and Fedel watched her sons. On the floor, Brando and the trainers educated Felix and Osmund on war weaponry and the handling of foreign hand-weapons by attacking the trainees with them.

"Felix is really quite forceful," his mother mused to Teva, "but Osmund is very light on his feet."

"He has the best defense," remarked Teva to Fedel. "Dodging a blow and running away preserve the man, if they do not preserve the nation."

"Oh, what do you know about that?" scoffed Nikeas. His cheekbones cut harsh across his visage, giving his pale pallor an almost dirty look. He had set his hands on the rail and was leaning there. Teva's long, rusty red hair undulated down her back in hundreds of braids, distracting always from her flower face, her serene gray eyes, her dainty nose, her tiny, coppery eyebrows. She lifted an eyebrow, still watching the tumbling and listening to the whacking and exclamations.

"You would think, dear sister," Teva said in a loud if not conspiratorial tone, "that my brother, Nikeas, *did* know something of battle, the way he crows."

"I know more of it than you do!"

"Fedel, did you hear that? Someone knows more of battle than I do!" Fedel just looked out of the corners of her eyes at Nikeas with a smirk. "I was sure that no one here under fifty had been to battle, except Brando."

Nikeas' face glassed over and his right hand twitched, almost imperceptibly. A moment later, Teva continued, "If I were a younger brother, I might be jealous, as well."

Through clenched teeth, Nikeas hissed, "How could you betray—?" Teva was at his side in a second, having unlinked from Fedel so that she could hang onto Nikeas' arm with both of hers, petting his upper arm with her palms and looking pleadingly into his averted face.

"Oh, don't be cross with me, Nikeas. I was only teasing. But I know it must be hard, sometimes, to be you. You'll have your day, some day. Perhaps you'll even have your own domain, somewhere." Nikeas' face softened as Teva cooed at him, and when she finished and he was looking sideways down at her, a muscle flexed in his jaw, creating a close-lipped underbite. His look told her not to be so free about the things she said, like that.

Her eyes pouted back at him, *I was only playing.*

Maram watched over Irene's shoulder as a peasant hurried from the castle gate, his gold hair tossing in the wind. She tilted her purple, heeled, silk slipper in the grass and waited for Irene to squirm. Irene stood immovable with a studied look of unconcern on her narrow, pale face. She kept her eyes boring into Maram's, even though Maram was looking nonchalantly over Irene's shoulder. Maram's pupils were just now moving ever so slowly in a sweep closer and closer to Irene's mass of platinum curls and silver-fox-fur cap. It was such a smart cap, once, but now Maram's velvety, wine colored bonnet was much smarter.

A muscle over Irene's high cheek-bone twitched, and Maram let her eyes settle back onto her companion. "Really, Irene. I don't know why the stony silence." Maram gave a toss of her many velvety, dark braids and sighed. Maram must have sighed once every three minutes since her twelfth birthday.

"Maram, I can't believe you expect me to grovel!"

Maram giggled, a profoundly false giggle. "Oh no, dear. My little Irene was never meant to *grovel*. But I don't understand why we can't use *your* carriage, too. The party is going to be much too big for our two barouches, and I can't expect the Staff Bearer's daughter to ride in the britska, now, can I?" Maram's brown eyes danced with mirth at the idea.

Irene reached out and firmly held on to Maram's forearm. "Maram! Of course not! But you *can't*—you just *can't* be unaware of our situation! With the carriage and the house and the maids and *everything!*" She addressed Maram with pleading eyes in a chill face. When Maram looked questions at her, Irene flung her dainty, gloved hands down to her sides and snorted out a light puff of air. "Oh! How can this be?"

Irene's eyes searched the soft lawn, saw without noting the other couples and groups of erect figures crisscrossing the grounds with great expanses between them. She was searching her mind, as well, for the way to properly say something that was not proper to say. "Maram," she asked curtly. "You have heard the rumors of us lately?"

"Oh, if you mean about your horse being made lame by—"

"No, not that." Nothing more presented itself. "Oh, very well, then. Maram, you are my oldest and dearest friend. I believe part of our friendship is founded on our similar status and our unswerving devotion to propriety and *rightness*. But I hope, right now, that there is *another* part of our friendship that is grounded in, well, something *else*."

Now Maram had a look of great concern on her face. "Irene! Do not on account of me perjure yourself!"

"Oh, Maram." Irene hardly missed a beat. "My house is falling in the world. How far it will fall, no one can yet say. I am not privy to the intricacies of *why* this is so; things about court and terrible rumors and ever since that robbery—well, I don't know the first thing about it, really. I have tried. I have tried all my usual methods—throwing glances and dropping hand cloths—but nothing is working. No one will tell me anything!" Irene stomped a dainty foot and gave a bitter laugh. Maram clung to Irene's elbow as Irene looked out over the green. Maram, in a breach of decorum, allowed a twist of agony to cross her face.

"Irene—" she breathed. "Please don't think I would ever choose propriety over our friendship. Not *our* friendship. It is the truest thing I have, really, when everything else might be snatched away!"

Ignoring her because, even though Maram was clearly supportive, she was also, deep down no doubt, enjoying the drama of this, Irene answered, "So no, I cannot lend you our barouche for the party. I have no barouche. Soon, I will have no more of *anything*, it seems."

"Can't anything be done?!" in a voice that registered as a high-pitched whisper. "Can't I do anything?"

"Dearest Maram, I can't imagine *what* hasn't been already tried," and she dabbed her hand cloth at the corner of her eye.

In the Dead of Winter

Society had curled up on itself for Farrah. It had closed the young, barren woman out of its beauty and graces. She who was once Farrah the Fair and the light of any ball, was now anathema. As far as Kentwend knew, infertility was catching. They kept away from her, were pitiless with their whispers and their averted gazes.

No one sent their daughters to her anymore, for who would send their little ladies to sulk in the shade of barrenness? Surely Farrah might brush against them during a lesson in needlepoint. She might give them the idea that being childless was acceptable. Whatever it was the courtiers were thinking or not thinking, they ostracized her completely. It is often that way with one who was once so revered. It's the unacknowledged jealousy.

But Farrah's husband had been blind to her horrific fate, her daily torture. He was so blind to their sterility that he forbade her to speak of securing their lineage with a purchased bastard or a borrowed nephew. He died blind.

And when he died, Farrah's land and her husband's title transferred to a cousin whom she barely knew. Certainly this cousin had no great love for her that he would think of her before his own wife and children. Yet he was already landed and had no need of a house, so he let Farrah live in her former home as a tenant. It was not meant to be a slight, but it was cruel because how could she keep it? How could she maintain it with no land, no income, and no husband or sons?

But Farrah would not beg or borrow.

Aren strode into her life before her husband's body was cold. She supposed he had been there all along, working for them, but Farrah had never needed to notice Aren. Now he came to her. He befriended her. Then slowly, he began talking of things that caught her breath in her throat. He offered her contacts and expertise. He was her only friend, and she saw a sort of twisted hope springing from his ideas. She felt trapped. She felt exhilarated. She felt tenacious.

They formed a partnership. From the beginning, their specialties were thievery, blackmail, and extortion. Over the years, Farrah became adept at her job as maestro. Oh, how she milked Aren dry so that she would still be allowed the guise of relaxing in her front window, sitting and watching the world so that the world might know she was still, after all, allowed a front window on the Road of Rustics and an afternoon for sitting. A lady, even so.

The underbelly of Kentwend feared and respected her, regarded Farrah and Aren as dangerous foes and powerful allies. All knew they were not beyond the reach of her tricks, her trades, the wrong side of her deals. She could move anywhere among them, do anything.

One day many years into her partnership with Aren, Farrah happened to remember a very old conversation, like someone talking through a wall. The memory was clouded with a sort of blinding light, and in it Farrah's old zither student, Irene, said her family had an old queen's slave bracelet. It did not take much work for Farrah to find Irene, to find her family, and to form a network around the Third Courtier.

The slave bracelet was stolen. It proved a worthy acquisition. Broken down, the gems would fetch considerable sums in the foreign market. The metal was fine and pure. Or would the story of the piece, left intact, fetch a higher price? Aren would have to travel abroad to find out. Then the Third Courtier did the unexpected: he was personally offended by the theft, convinced there was a mole among his household, and pushed the matter with the castle. A carriage boy disappeared. A maid went suddenly mute. And the Courtier pushed harder, bought his own respect among the underground with cash and modest appointments on his farms to the south.

Mildly afraid of apprehension, Farrah and Aren sat on the slave bracelet. In fact, on intelligence that the Third Courtier had been sniffing very close to their back door—metaphorically speaking—they decided to lay low for a bit. They had lost some of their contacts now to the Third Courtier. They suffered a lack of stability for the first time in their careers. And it made them mad.

Like any lady would, Farrah retaliated by slandering the Third Courtier good and thick. She tossed out wild rumors and seedy tales into the chaff of Kentwend tongues, and stories and proofs up to the highest levels of Northwyth judiciary and society, the whitest and silkiest of ears. She was out for revenge. Only then would she regain her security and keep her reputation—a double-edged sword—sharp and dangerous.

She aimed high: she wanted the Third Courtier's complete demise. If her plan worked, he would lose his title and with it his land and his home. And darned if it wasn't actually working, so far. There were but a few more well-placed pushes, and the Courtier's family would topple. It was enough to make her giddy.

This afternoon, Farrah the Barren was alone. Aren the Lackey was out on Farrah's questionable errands. Farrah sat in her front room and kept a firm face, while her body trembled under a fur throw. She could never forgive herself for trembling or for any other weakness. She had been barren—inexcusable. Her husband died without progeny, even one purchased from a harlot or borrowed from a brother—inexcusable. Farrah alone would uphold this house, this space in society—damn her husband's cousin who now owned her name, her land. She would not tremble when her methods affected those around her. She had to have a spine to begin this, and she would have a spine until the end.

Aren came in the front door. Farrah had missed his approach, lost in thought. That meant she had not been paying attention to the comings and goings on the street. An empire built on watching and holding details and she was letting her mind wander!

Aren shed his overcoat and hat and came into the room where Farrah sat by the window, wrapped up against the freeze that seeped through the many panes. "Farrah, wouldn't you like me to re-start the fire?"

Farrah didn't move. "You know, Aren, I was just sitting here, letting my thoughts float away on me like a schoolgirl."

"M'lady?"

"Oh, nothing, Aren."

Farrah sat in silence, Aren stood biding his time. After a while, he said, "I have good news." Farrah twisted around in her chair. She encouraged him to continue with her eyes. "The former Third Courtier has defaulted on his home and title. They intend to fight the royal authority for a right to stay in the Outer Circle, but Regar has said it is already decided: he will be denied. The best they can hope for is to move outward and farm,"—Farrah gave a snort—"or take what is left, patch it together to look impressive, and march into some other town looking to advise a king or tutor a princess.

Their few remaining friends have told them to consider the latter."

"When will his fate be decided?"

"Not at least until the spring, if the spring ever comes this year."

Aside, she said without any investment, "It is a long, difficult winter." The gears of Farrah's mind turned. "Alright then, I don't suppose it is too early to gather new investments." It was the pet phrase they used for extorting the vulnerable into regular payments in support of their power. "Who's on our list?"

Aren thought for a moment, his thin finger on his pointed chin. "I believe we had discussed Nora the Girl Widow."

"Yes, I believe she'll do nicely. Go and see her tomorrow."

¤

"Do you think The Queen's hair is shining red gold, down to her knees, like they say?"

"Or that her green eyes could pierce through your heart with a single glance?"

"Or she could read your mind?"

"What do they mean by *piercing* the heart, exactly? Like *stabbing*? Or more like *effecting*? Would you die, or never love again?"

Four sets of eyes swung around the campfire and settled on Raban. The others were used to his childishness—Raban's mind was many years younger than his body, many years younger than any of theirs—so his philosophic musings were sudden and baffling. Raban responded by slowly chewing the last piece of venison in his stew and swabbing his chunk of bread in his pewter bowl. He looked up at a pitch-black night sky shot through with stars in blotches and streaks of multitudes. The fire crackled and popped. Sparks shot upward out of leaping flames. A wolf sang.

Raban stood up and stretched one leg out and then the other.

He turned his back to the fire and mumbled. "Bedtime," he said, rubbing at his eye with his balled fist. He hated to leave the warm circle and walk the paces to the wagon. He was the biggest of the travelers, had the most brawn, like an elephant-calf among men. He shook black curls out of his shadowy eyes and waited for Musa to move behind him.

"Alright, Raban." Musa gathered her bowl, cup, and spoon into the folds of her cloak and dress, blooming with underskirts. She passed by Raban and hurried off into the night and into the wagon, alone. The wagon creaked and shifted even under her slight weight. The door thwacked shut behind her and then Raban listened to the sounds of Musa preparing the stove, cleaning out yesterday's ash, filling its round belly with kindling and wood, starting the fire with flint.

She appeared at the doorway, barely a movement in the dark. Raban could see the starlight glinting off her cheek and reflecting in her midnight eyes. "Raban! The flints are taking too long. Just bring me some fire before I freeze to death."

The three other men were still and silent around the fire. Seti, Raban's cousin, held his boots almost in the flames and his hand rested on his knee, casually holding his mess tin. His long, black hair was tied off with a thong, except where it came loose to stick to his dark whiskers. Drakon pulled hard at the warmth of a pipe stuffed with djerweed. Blaise's ghost white eyes were wide, watching the fire. All three of them, like the other two in the wagon, were approaching middle age but looked harder than that, touched by the elements and the difficult life of the peasantry compounded by itinerancy.

Seti looked up to see Raban standing, his jaw slack, staring into the fire. "Go on, Raban," Seti prodded. "There's a stick, there." He nodded at a long switch propped against a stone beside the fire. "We need to heat the wagon so we can *all* get some sleep."

Blaise leaned back into an attentive recline. His voice was hard and tinny as he said, "We should be in Northwyth by tomorrow. We may encounter some resistance, but we'll be convincing." He eyed the three other men around the fire. His look said he was unimpressed, but they would do. "And then it's Kentwend before the month is out. We should be in place before the ground is soft enough to bury anyone who should die, even a queen."

¤

The rolling hills between the town of Kentwend and Branderby Woods were frosted over and blue. They reflected back a white sky in harsh glints and razor-fine curves. The grasses and last year's crops had been harvested and ploughed, dug up, and flattened by the howling winds and the weight of snows that fell heavy and then blew in drifts down to the valleys. Or perhaps it was the despair that the whole landscape was feeling from the incessant cold.

Daina scanned her eyes over the barren spaces past her farm. The only thing to cut the white, the blue, and the glare, was her garden gate. Planks in disrepair broke the drifts of snow in clean pools of shadow. She looked north, and there was nowhere to set her eyes. She looked south, and Cecily's cabin nestled against her homestead to begin a line of dwellings that swelled up the hill in an undulating, dotted line.

A road hugged the line of dwellings and continued up around the side of Daina's farm before forcing the traveler to decide between burrowing into the farms and then the town, or heading— quite literally—for the hills. A man walked up the road that led to Daina's. Daina knew this man's gait, knew exactly who it was when he was just a wavering, wisp of a mirage coming down from Gretl's Way. It was Conover, and he came around here so much over the past five years that the scandal that had begun with his visiting "the widow" in her mourning clothes had long since become the scandal of him visiting her so often and for so long. What did the Storykeeper want with that scrap of a used-up widow, anyhow? Guess they were about as odd and empty-headed as each other.

Come to think of it, though, Daina hadn't seen as much of him this winter. Every fool soul was buried deep in their hovel or home, burning everything in sight and wrapping their feeble bodies in all the clothes they owned at once. It was that cold. And the wind! Daina tugged at her scarf and pulled it further up around her face. All that one could see of Daina's smudged, ruddy, round face were her thin, dark eyes.

Daina had been alone out in the ethereal landscape with the domiciles all winter. They looked abandoned except for the smoke that curled from their stovepipes and chimneys. Of course, she wasn't *always* outside or she would have frozen to death, but she was outside more often than anyone else, even the snotty children. She was keeping away from the Drunk.

Daina clucked to herself, sardonically. How long ago had he been given that title? If only it had been *before* Daina had married him, before they had started copulating, the babies squalling and looking for food. Now the children helped out some, half-dressed in patched-together rags and home-cobbled shoes, picking up jobs appropriate for slight people, for bone-thin physiques and shoulders weak with the dregs of their last sickness, the blue bruises in lines across their backs, on their poor, skeletal arms.

The Drunk was a kind name for him. He was far worse.

Daina winced. What was the use in coming out here if she was going to stand here and torture *herself*?

Conover turned at Cecily's gate. He raised a heavily-wrapped arm and hand at Daina, but she just stood and glared at him. Normally her glare would have been accompanied by some biting words and a back-and-forth. Today, both their mouths were wrapped round with their itchy, wool scarves and beaded with hot vapors of breath.

In town, Conover had broken out in a sweat. At the edge of the farmland, the sweat had chilled and he was in danger of freezing. But he was getting to Cecily's, if it was the last thing he did. He had been laying groundwork for two months. He was going to honor The Queen and Cecily and begin it before Sonnetide.

He threw his body against the door and thunked his fist after his body. He heard scuffling, and when Cecily opened the door, he tripped into the golden glow and the warm blast of air on his face. "Conover!" she gasped. She hurried to help him unwind his head and peel the wrappings from his hands as he deeply inhaled the smell of burning sandalwood, cinnamon, and sweet hay. Cecily was alone today, as usual. Her loneliness both ached him in the chest and relieved him.

He didn't speak for a while, and Cecily didn't require him to, didn't say anything herself. She took his coverings and cloak while he sat down on a wooden chair to pull off his wet, leather boots. Cecily busied herself around the one room that comprised the entire living area with a small loft. She heated a kettle and shook tea leaves into a chipped, earthenware cup. The steam rose up into her wearied face, and she pursed her lips to blow on it. The heat lifted the tendrils of baby hair that lined her forehead.

"I'm sorry about the puddle," Conover said as she handed him the tea. He looked down at the spreading darkness on the sand-polished wood planking. She looked at him and smiled. "And I'm sorry we're here alone, again." Then they both smiled, conspiratorially. People *would* talk.

In the weighty silence that followed, Cecily found conversation that matched Conover's current gravity. "You know why I love magic? Why I care so much about it?" It was always like this for them, picking up an old conversation like they had just paused for a moment. Conover shook his head, no. She set her cup down and shifted so that she was looking to a distance beyond the walls of the cottage. She took a moment to continue. "When I was a girl,

The Queen passed here," she gestured toward a front yard that they could not see and a road running under the ice and snow. "I remember thinking about the stories my own mother had told me when I was a child, before she died. The stories of The Queen, The Angel, The Sage, and King Jaden, the most miraculous ones; those always seemed to be her favorites. Stories that never could have happened but that every child believed with all their heart and every mother recited. Did mothers believe them? As I grew older, mothers and children were relegated more and more into the realm of the elderly, the simple, and the evil, unable to distinguish truth from fiction with their facile minds.

"But I wasn't a mother yet. I was no longer a child. So I stood and waited for The Queen as I wondered. And then she approached with her train and her fanfare. I threw daisies before her carriage, and she looked on the peasants and waved. And when she waved, the ring on her finger caught in the sun, and it burst into fire." She headed him off when he shifted uncomfortably. "I don't mean it was actual flame, but the reality wasn't any less appalling. It shot out an intense beam of light, a hundred times more intense than the sun, brilliant and red. And it made a sound: a high, thin humming. And everyone was amazed. Just for a second, the ring had been unable to contain the magical half-seed inside, and a reflective bit of inane magic—a miracle—burst forth.

"It was, of course, the answer to my question. But I knew I couldn't live that way, not at least until I had my own children to regale with *fairy tales*." She spit the word out. "So I kept that story, all the stories, here," she laid her fist on her chest with a light thump, "and I spent an adulthood, a life that incidentally was not my own but stolen from another woman," her eyes clouded over before clearing again, "wondering about truth and reality, truth and fact. Truth.

"It was part of what drew me to you," she said. Conover met her eyes, now completely softened. "You're the *Storykeeper*. I thought you surely must understand that fact is not truth, nor is reality, or vice versa. Truth is a creature all its own, and it can be found in many places, even in magic. In miracles. Even in stories."

"I've disappointed you?"

"No, you have never disappointed me." She blushed. "You have been the best thing in my life. How could you have disappointed me?"

"But I don't believe the way you need me to."

"I think you will."

"And what if I don't? What if I never have the heart to?"

"Mmm." She turned her face away from him to think about this. "I guess it doesn't matter. We're not…"

"Cecily—" he interrupted her. Something in his voice alarmed Cecily, and she sat up straight in her own chair, pulled from her reverie. He cleared his throat. Then he did it again. "Cecily—"

"Is everything okay?"

"Yes. Well, I mean… I hope it will be. I mean, Cecily, I have to ask you something."

"Yes?" Now she was fully engaged, and yet the heaviness, the wizardry of the previous conversation pervaded each breath, each syllable. Was nothing just to be his own, just Conover's? Was it always to also belong to storytelling?

Conover turned his whole body toward her, leaned in just an inch or two. Cecily flushed, but she didn't look away. That was one of the best things about Cecily; she might seem malleable, meek, but she never shied away from him or from the honest truth. She was looking at him so expectantly! Her sweet face—he knew every line and contour—set on him.

"Cecily, would you marry me if I asked you? I mean—would it make sense?"

Never in his many sleepless nights had Conover imagined what happened next: Cecily, the Baker's Widow, jumped from her seat with her hands at her mouth and fell on Conover with a powerful, smothering embrace. She clung to his neck, and Conover felt everything had been worth it.

◇

Nora yanked at the few feathers left in the chicken. She stuffed them into a sack hanging beside the counter and turned to butcher the carcass. There was a knock at the door. Nora wiped her hands roughly on her house apron, scrubbing at the film and blood as she approached the door. She opened it and stood framed by the jambs. She was neat and tidy, clean-faced, no hair out of place beneath her winged bonnet. Her ruby lips stood out in her light, narrow face, around small, rabbity teeth. Her eyes were cows' eyes, brown and calm to match her brown, calm hair. She stood almost two heads shorter than Aren, who was rather a tall and lanky fellow, a perfect match for Farrah.

"Hello, um…"

"Aren, Farrah's Lackey."

"Hello." She gave him a placating smile. "Aren, Farrah's Lackey. Is there something I can help you with?"

"As a matter of fact, there is. May I come in?" It was clearly not a question.

"Of course. I should shut this door against the wind." Aren stepped out of the cold and into Nora's neat home. It was small and poor, but Nora had an eye for things, made things nicer than what they were. Her reed basket's pattern was brighter and more intricate than most. Her clay baking bowls were rounded smoother at the bottom and painted a rustier shade of red, each with an inset of carved shell. In the middle of the room hung a mobile made from ribbon and pieces of shattered glass. On a summer day, it caught the sunlight and made dancing beam-spots.

"Can I get you something?" Nora asked. Aren noted that

she looked every bit as young as she was. Her face was uncreased, fresh. She barely had breasts beneath her pleated smock. The Girl Widow.

"No. Please don't bother."

What did Nora know about Aren? About Farrah? Clearly Aren belonged in the Outer Circle of Kentwend. His leather boots were neatly cut, formed to his foot, and lined with a spotted fur she could not identify. His coat, too, was tailored and a brilliant scarlet, lined with another foreign fur. And leather gloves, soft as morning snow, fitted to his slender fingers! Gold at his neck. Coiffed hair, buried beneath a tall, velvety, winter hat. Long features to match his length. Pale blue eyes sizing her up just as she was appraising him.

Farrah the Barren was an infamous personage in the world of courtiers and kings, gossiped about religiously by the peasants. Nothing good was said about her. Fear permeated the rumor mill. With that reputation, Nora hardly wanted Aren to be here, in her home.

"Well, what can I help you with, then?" She gestured toward the kitchen table. "I'm in the middle of preserving a chicken."

"One of your own, I suppose?" Aren raised his eyebrows at the farthest end of the one-room home, where a gate demarcated pens for the goats, the cow, the rabbits, and a shelf for the chickens. They were all quietly making animal sounds, light rustlings and the occasional clucking, domestic noises for small homes in the wintertime.

"Yes, that is how we do it here. I suppose you have yours brought in on a silver tray, dressed and glistening with duck fat?"

"Yes. I do." His eyebrows had lifted at her last sentence. He was usually not met with sauciness among the peasantry.

"Again, sir, we come to it. What, besides comparisons of the culinary habits of the peasant versus the courtier, can I help you with?"

"Now now, girl." He couldn't help it; he was unsteadied by

her. He had expected her to be submissive and dumb and to know her place in society. Apparently she was rather bright and assertive. "Don't get yourself in a twist. I have a proposal. Perhaps, if you are careful with it, you too can have your chicken brought in on a silver platter."

"I doubt that. And must I—?"

"You must. Now listen." Aren took a step toward Nora, using his height to look down his aquiline nose at her. "*We* know that your life, as the Girl Widow, is not ultimately sustainable. Your husband—God rest his soul—was not with you long enough to leave you either relational provision or heavy with child."

Nora also took a step toward him, her eyes flashing and her cheeks flushed. She interrupted, "We didn't even finish our honeymoon!" by which she meant the three days after a marriage when peasants weren't required to work. "Of course he couldn't—but it's enough, anyhow! Enough for me. My husband was a good man."

"Oh, don't fret, child. I *understand* that your husband was *unable* to account for his sudden death. Who would understand that better than Farrah the Barren?" He left a pause, for effect, and Nora just stood and watched, not revealing whether or not she knew of Farrah's past disappointments. "So, again to the proposal." He hurried back through the intro, as if getting to a part of a memorized speech where he had left off. "Weknowthatyourlife, astheGirlWidow, isnotultimatelysustainable. Yourhusband, Godresthissoul wasnotwithyoulongenoughtoleaveyouwithprovision. So, Farrah the Barren has lovingly and graciously decided to become your benefactor. She will offer you *protection* in return for monetary donations."

"What?!"

Aren's hand shot out in a barely discernable flash, lightly pressing the palm of the soft, leather glove hard against her mouth. He shushed her.

"And your monetary donations will be returned to you, in

course, multiplied. You will find that Farrah is a discerning investor. Of course, you must understand that her protection would include immunity from the allegations that you—how shall we put this delicately?—*helped* your husband transit from this life to the next."

Nora stepped back from Aren's hand, wrenching her head to the side to dodge him. "But I never! I would never! No one would believe it!"

Aren let a smirk spread slowly across his face. "Oh, wouldn't they? You'll find that with the right persuasion, they will." Nora now stared with her mouth hanging open. "And with *proof.*" His look told Nora that if he didn't already have some such ludicrous thing, it could be made to appear very easily. "Of course, Farrah's protection spreads to making that proof disappear, as well as that pesky story."

At the Appearance of Ground Under the Snow

When Nrom the Smithy's Wife had been great with child, the midwife laid a papery hand on Nrom's distended stomach and told her it felt like two babies at war; the evil eye was upon them. When Nrom the Smithy's Wife had gone into labor early and fierce, the first child, a boy, had been named Brom. The second child, a girl, had been named Bricteva. But Nrom's labor was still in progress, and the third child had been named Butrus.

Triplets were regarded so sideways and with such portents that they could never become smithies or candlers or soapsmiths. They were born—with just a little ingenuity and creativity—to be street performers. Unlike Nrom, who was stalwart and thick, the Triplets were compact and sinewy, tight and hard and waiting in energy to unfurl. Brom would become a world class contortionist. Bricteva could dance like a zephyr and sing like a lark. Butrus became a magician.

Where the Triplets went, crowds gathered, and it didn't take long for them to catch an opportunist in their wake: Panther the Pickpocket. The Triplets were just the rough and tumble sort to welcome Panther into their confidences, and the four of them barely aged as they passed twenty and edged toward thirty. It was fun, apparently, to have the evil eye on you.

The Storykeeper's wedding wouldn't have been celebrated without inviting Brom, Bricteva, and Butrus. Many of the musicians and entertainers among the peasants of Kentwend were invited to each and every wedding, as well as the best and most generous of home cooks and the most privileged and gracious among the townsfolk.

The tent among the hills across the road from Cecily's cottage was filled with a confusion of noises and sights. The Triplets were among the revelers. Brom bent himself in half and worked his leg into a sort of loop above his head, to the "Oooh!"s of those gathered. Bricteva danced in a corner near a supporting post. She circled a tambourine around her flying, long, brown hair as she sang to the raucous musical accompaniment of a lutist. Butrus walked among the toasters and dancers asking, "What's that behind your ear?" Panther—uninvited, officially—was doing what he did best.

A woman plucked daintily at a small harp. A couple of geriatric men battled with their fiddles. At one end of the tent, a play was performed outside in the cold sun. At the other end, a puppeteer was surrounded by attentive children and rung round again, more loosely, by children running among the thawing grasses, spattering mud across their frocks, their clogs and flashes of stockinged legs blurring by.

Barrels of mead were tapped and flowing. Mismatched tables, dragged from the neighbors' houses, were laden with food: stacks of golden rolls; heaps of sweetpies; whole, burnished fowl; and game carved open and already emptied of the choicest meat. It smelled, first of all, like mud and an extremely welcome spring wind. It smelled, also, of roasted meat, fresh bread, sharp spices, pungent, pickled vegetables, and people—their hair, their woolen clothes, their leather shoes, their breath and sweat.

Cecily and Conover were at the very center of the tent, clinging to each other, not to be wrenched apart by the revelries. They grinned, blushed, yelled, were forced into doing a jig, Conover's arm pumped while an inebriated farmer wished him all the best and claimed Conover had always been his favorite townsperson. Kentwend knew how to celebrate a thing, and weddings were an accumulation of everyone's participation and giftings. There had been many objections to this marriage, but not any surprise when Conover announced his choice of wife. There would be many wagging heads and tongues in the years to come, but a Northwyth wedding was a thing without gall.

◻

The local players—Aesop, Elpis, Zosimus, Saga, and Hero—performed a comedy. Only comedies were performed at weddings. The play portrayed a damsel, a knight, a stepmother, a boy, and a villain. Hero delivered a line in falsetto. "Take this creature away from me!" He swung a wide-sleeved arm out to the side while bringing the other arm up to his forehead in comic distress. He gazed out into the tent as he stood statuesque, waiting for the next several lines to be spoken.

He watched the pulsating crowd, as well as individual frames of someone laughing, someone gorging on a mutton leg, a man leaning in for a stolen kiss. When Hero delivered his next line, the man was being slapped. Hero recited, "That is all I can handle! Away with me!" and swooped away from the plot of grass in front of the curtains and beams the actors were using as a backdrop. He looped around back of the curtains and stood there, hidden, blotting at his makeup with his top skirt.

Beside the backstage ran the narrow end of the tent and a table that ended at a heap of mead barrels. Wine bottles and glass liquor flasks dotted the table, each bottle stamped with the insignia of the family who produced it—and would be coming back for their glassware. Few bottles remained unopened. Most bottles were empty, a purpley or golden puddle at the bottom. Several bottles lay on their side. Two had fallen into the grass and mud.

A wide, imposing man with a ring of brown hair and a snub nose over his unruly beard stood, draining a bottle of wine, while Hero watched. When the last bit dripped into his mug, he lapped at the mouth of the bottle with his tongue. Another man approached and slapped at the man's elbow, threatening to disrupt the fresh-poured liquor. "Rufus!" he called. "Come 'ere, old boy!" The two withdrew from the table into the shade of a lone elm tree, where they were alone in the crowd.

Alone except for the man dressed as a stepmother crouched in the shadows and folds of the curtains, waiting for his cue.

"Rufus, there has been talk," Kori grumbled. His head lolled side to side, his tongue thick, and his eyes unsettled as they scanned the churning masses. "The Queen is going to die, and soon. There was talk at the last meeting of the Band of Farmers. She'll be buried in the family crypt under the castle." Rufus' head spun at all of this disconnected information. Perhaps, he thought, it was the old wine. Kori's concluding question didn't help. "What good will all those riches do her there?"

Rufus said, "Humph," and appeared to consider this metaphysical quandary.

Kori dropped a heavy arm onto Rufus' closest shoulder. The shoulder was a good foot above Kori's. "I think someone's going to try to take all that gold." He ended his speech looking at the side of Rufus' face. They stood like this a few moments, then Kori removed his arm, punched Rufus gaily in the side, and teetered off, back to the merriment.

Rufus stood brooding, massaging his brow with thick fingers, while behind him, Hero too thought. What good *would* all those riches do there? They both stared absently at the table of bottles. A bottle rattled, and they both looked to it. It continued to rattle with a beat that grew more frenetic. What a way for the wind to behave. Could a breeze be doing that? Then a pile of used wax seal swirled up into a little dance before falling off the table's edge. And then all the bottles began to rise. They did not go altogether, but the lighter ones first, and both Hero and Rufus thought it was a trick of the light. But they rose higher and higher, until they stood about a foot off the table, and gathered into a chain dance. They bobbed and teetered both akward and graceful, like puppets, round and round the circle once or twice. Then they slowed and settled back to the table.

Hero heard his cue repeated loudly, and Rufus wondered whose mead had been let to spoil.

¤

Here and there in the town of Kentwend, the streets opened up into spaces that allowed for a well, through-traffic, or a market. Several tables or booths had been stationed around a square in north Kentwend since daybreak. A small crowd bustled. Vendors called their wares. A farmer herded goats through the street and a baker balanced a basket of round loaves on his hip as he walked the crowd, jingling his pouch of pfennigs.

A woman hiding her enormous, distended belly under tucks and folds of brown fabric, leaned forward to peer down at a neat pile of baubles arranged on a deflated cloth bag. Even though these were the plainer pieces meant for sale to the peasants for special occassions, the hair adornments were intricate and beautiful. She wanted to touch them, but the ground was much too far away. There was no bending for her at this stage.

"Adornment for your beautiful daughter?" The woman followed the feet that straddled the bag up a long skirt and to the plain, brown face of the seller. She was small as a child.

Without realizing it, the woman's free hand settled on her stomach and rubbed distractedly at it. "Oh," she said. "I think it's to be a son." She smiled kindly at the seller.

"Y'never can tell. Adornment for his bride, then?"

"No, not today."

Another woman sidled up to the first, a younger woman. "Come now, cuz. Don't bother Trecora. She be touching the hair of dead people. She's no good for chat."

"I *buy* hair!" gasped Trecora, blushing. "From *alive* people! Some of this here is royal hair! And I can tell you you're no better'n me."

The younger woman ignored her, and turned to her cousin, saying, "Can't be too careful with the baby coming." Then she reached out a hand and settled it beside the first woman's, resting on the bulge. She had been about to steer the woman away from the stall when the baby underneath the women's hands kicked. They looked up into each other's eyes and smiled.

"Does it hurt?"

"A bit. Not in the way you think."

"Is it wonderful?"

"Yes. I suppose so."

The young woman closed her eyes, retreating to thoughts about the baby or about her own body or her own possible motherhood. Suddenly she jumped back, as if she had touched fire. "I... I saw something," she said, startled by herself.

"You dreaming?" The first woman's smile turned sly,

conspiratorial.

"No! No! I really *saw* something!" By the end of the sentence, she was screaming, and people were looking over.

"Alright. Okay." Her cousin tried to calm her, but the younger woman's eyes grew wild, and she wrung her hands in agitation.

"You were here!" she yelled, indicating the square around them and the well at its center. "And it was Royal Deluge Day! The royal family was drinking from the well..." She searched the air for her words, "And there was a warm wind from the south..."

"Shhh. It's okay." The woman gave a concerned look over her shoulder at the gathering, nosy neighbors. But the young woman seemed not to notice her, even though she spoke to her.

"She's a girl, cousin!" The younger woman pointed at the older woman's abdomen. "And then it was years later, here again! And she was nearly a woman. And she came to buy a bridal adornment from... from her!" She indicated Trecora, a note of derision in her voice, offended that she too had been in the vision. "She was going to marry the Storykeeper!" She broke off, panting as if she had just run the length of the Dacidava.

The older woman smiled crookedly as she said, "Who? That old man? He'll be dead and gone before I have a grown daughter."

"No. No. He was younger." She seemed confused by this and yet defiant. The woman, at last, managed to envelop her cousin into a fold of her shawl and escort her away. But many had heard. They whispered together snatches of the conversation.

Rufus stood so amazed that a little boy filched a bun out of his basket without him noticing. Hero leaned into Zosimus and asked, "We have prophetesses, again?" and raised his eyebrows. Nikeas, hidden in the crowd beneath a cloak, watched in amused silence as the two women scurried away, until a movement at the entering road called his attention, and a trumpet blast rent the air.

The herald called into the square. "Make way! Your royal family, Princess Fedel of Northwyth, and her sons, Prince Felix and

Prince Osmund!" Nikeas disappeared in a swirl of fabric around the corner of a blacksmith's shop.

Prince Felix rolled his eyes at his younger brother.

"Must we always go about like this?"

"I like it!" Osmund still had the smooth skin of a baby and a glint of innocence in his wide, brown eyes.

"Well I don't."

"You don't like anything anymore." Osmund frowned at Felix, but Felix was looking around, not bothering to hear his brother. Felix had spotted a few peasants his own age nearby. They were chatting animatedly to each other, and one of the girls was quite pretty, her skirts rather short for her age. Very slim ankles and tiny feet. Most of the peasants had feet like boats. From all the walking, he supposed.

"Felix!" Fedel's voice snapped him from his reverie. She was calling him to continue around the square with the entourage, and when he looked at her, her hand was extended to a kneeling peasant, touching her forehead to the lavender-scented, ivory-colored skin of the back of Fedel's hand. Fedel's voice had drawn the attention of the peasant teenagers, and when Felix looked back at them, he found the pretty girl looking into his face, her lips in an "Oh!" As soon as their eyes met, she curtsied low and bowed her head, breaking eye contact. She stubbornly refused to stratighten herself before he looked away, so he did, striding after the others.

Would it take all his life to get used to being a future king?

¤

Seti sat on the plank seat at the front of the wagon. The reigns lay across the tops of his blackened leather gloves and hung down into his loose fists. Raban sat beside him. Sitting out front always calmed Raban, even more so if Musa were up front. When Seti,

Raban and Musa sat side by side, the giant, box wagon swaying, creaking, and rattling as it dipped into the road's holes, the forest stretching out around them full of twittering birds, dashing foxes, and a never-ending green, it was almost like a family—some sort of giant-babied, harlot-mothered, ugly-fathered family.

Seti snorted out a sneering chuckle to himself. Musa was in the back now as had been required by Blaise and Drakon. It had been winter for ages.

Thank the Lord that be for this breeze, the first thing to come of spring. The ground was still hard and seeped chill, but the week had been filled with that teasing of warmness, the melting of the snows, the fragrance of things coming alive. And there, off to the east and directly where they were slowly headed, a break in the trees and glintings of sky between the branches and trunks.

Seti took his right hand from the reigns and thumped against the wagon wall with his arm and fist. "Hey, you!" he yelled out, his voice gravelly with disuse. He waited until the wooden hatch at the top of the wagon popped open and Drakon's head appeared.

"What?"

"Big clearing. As wide as I can see. Think it might be Kentwend?"

"Might be, yeah." Drakon pulled his head back in to confer with Blaise.

Yesterday morning, they had been traveling in pleasant weather, the wagon lurching, creaking, and jangling between the close branches and trunks. Very early, they passed through a river that still carried small, sparkling floes of ice. On the east of it, Seti spotted a lone traveler ahead on the road. He had meant to keep it quiet, but Blaise chose that moment to move to the coach box. For a minute, they thought they might rob the stranger, but then decided it would be best for the law not to precede them to Kentwend.

They gained on the man. He seemed not to hear the

commotion they made, or their horses snorting in his ear, so he kept to the middle of the road, walking slowly forward, placing his staff gently down with each step. Blaise nodded and held out his hands for the reigns while Seti halted the horses and jumped down to the ground.

"Old man!" he called. He walked forward around the man, giving him a decent berth. "Old man!"

When The Sage saw the crinkly-eyed foreigner with the dirty riding gloves and sleek, black hair, he stopped walking and turned round. He smiled brightly at the halted living-wagon, the stamping horses salivating at their bits, and the three heads poking out of the wagon's shutter. "Excuse me, sirs and madam! I must have been very deep in thought!"

"You don't know if you were thinking?" snickered Drakon.

"It's like living in two towns, you know. Sometimes you forget exactly where you left off."

Seti, standing beside the man, was amused by him. Blaise spat to the side of the wagon. "Clear the road, old man."

"Why certainly. I am only too aware of the flibflobbery the five of you might come up with to overpower me deep in the uninhabited wilderness. Do you know these woods?"

"Sure." Drakon spoke again. "These are the Branderby Woods outside of the town of Kentwend in the kingdom of Northwyth. We're on our way to Kentwend." Blaise shot Drakon a cold glance and Drakon quailed. He dropped out of sight and Musa sighed contempt after him.

The Sage charged ahead with his good-humored conversation. "So that's what they call this place nowadays?"

"And for a hundred years, at least!" Seti almost laughed. "It's quite famous!"

"I suppose you come for the same reason I do?"

Blaise cut in quickly. "We don't share our plans with you, old man."

"Oh, I see. Don't any of you read cards? Tea leaves? Talk to animals?" At this, The Sage extended the hand that did not carry his staff and a bird flew to it, settled on the curve of his palm where it became finger. He regarded the bird with the same attention and patience he was giving these travelers. "You and I won't be the only ones coming to town. Not with such magic at work." His eyes glinted as they peeked over the bird's head, looking to the travelers' faces as if they were open books.

Blaise stood in the box. "All right, old man! Out of our way, then. Go talk magic to your birds in a ditch, or we'll make you move."

The Sage strode calmly to the side of the road and a few feet into the brush. Seti mounted the wagon, and they moved on.

"Who do you suppose that was?" Seti asked Blaise, since there was no one else there.

"An old fool, obviously. Must live nearby."

"Oh no, I don't think so."

Blaise exhaled his opinion of Seti's reasoning.

Seti persisted. "He was a traveler, like us, but without all the trappings. And he was both old and young at the same time. His staff was... well, sort of remarkable. And he had a king's ring, did you notice?"

"King's rings don't exist. And if they did, you wouldn't know how to spot them."

"At any rate, I'm real glad we weren't robbing him. Would have been more trouble than it was worth, for sure."

"An old man and a bird?" Blaise's sneer carried into his voice. "Tell you what. We won't be so kind to the next old fart we find alone in the woods."

But later that day, close to twilight, when—with Blaise still up front with Seti—they were discussing where to stop, they met a traveler and Blaise dared not carry out his proclamation. Up ahead on the road walked a familiar, cloaked profile. This time he turned to see them.

"What?!? Have you been driving us in circles all day?" Blaise reached back as if to strike Seti, and Seti threw up his arm in defense of his head.

"Oh, no! No!" called The Sage. "You've made a day's progress toward Kentwend! You're nearly there! And apparently, so am I."

Blaise stared slack-jawed at the man. From under his elbow, Seti asked, "But you couldn't have walked as fast as all that, sir."

"Apparently I was moving too slow for fate."

And on those parting words, Blaise reached over and grabbed the reigns, then smacked them to get the horses moving. The horses jostled forward and The Sage hurried to the side, where he stood smiling and waving goodbye to them.

The living-wagon traveled quite a distance in the deepening darkness before Blaise would settle. Then he roused the other travelers, after only a few hours' sleep, to continue. Most of the day, as he drove, Seti's tired mind churned disjointed thoughts about the stranger, before it finally settled into the usual daydreams of Raban and Musa as companions. Then Seti spotted the clearing through the trees.

Within ten minutes the wagon was through the edge of the Branderby Woods and easing down a hill among many bare hills. In the distance rose the castle of Northwyth, which dissolved at its base into the town of Kentwend and eased out into huts dotting the rolling farmlands. The castle glinted in the sun, blinking back gold at the travelers as the sun set behind their backs. The farmlands were already in shadow, and Seti could see, directly ahead on the road, a tent at a crossroads.

"Look, Seti!" Raban thrust a finger out at the tent. "A party!"

Indeed, the tent was strung with paper lanterns lit against the setting sun, surrounded by dots of cheerful fires. Music and voices rose to them on the intermittent breeze, along with the smell of roasting meat. Seti's stomach turned over, empty with longing.

"Looks like we've a wedding to go to." Seti flashed a grin over at Raban, and Raban clapped his hands.

¤

Jaden strode down the hall, the firelight from the wall sconces flickering off his set face, his narrowed brows, his steady eyes. He thought to himself, *Just this afternoon she sat over the presentation of the Storykeeper's new wife.* And indeed, The Queen had sat on her throne, her crown in place, her robe draped over rail-thin arms, and her silver hair braided and set running over her shoulder and down into her lap. Her cheeks had been more flushed, her lips more red, than was usual. Even her eyes had glittered more fervently. Had her constricted tears been merely a watering of the eyes? It would have been just like her to cry such a dignified tear when Conover presented his wife, a slender, brown, middle-aged woman looking radiant through all the knocks the years had given her. The woman had had a fresh, happy feel about her, the first spring bride on her wedding day in her ivory and blue wedding dress with lace at the neck and cuffs.

Cecily had kissed the hem of The Queen's scarlet robe at the pure white, fur lining, and The Queen had declined her head with a warm smile.

The sound of Jaden's heavy slippers on the thick runners, the sound of his snorting breath, and the whispering of his night robe trailing behind him were the only sounds in the hall until he approached the door. Then he could hear voices behind it.

He threw open the door without knocking, without pausing. It was too large and heavy to go far, but it scattered people around in the dim of the room. Jaden noticed they were all knotted close to the door, as if afraid to go further in. "Out!" he yelled, and they seeped out behind him as he continued his march across the rug past the strategy table to the bedside.

A few attendants lingered by the bedside, despite his exclamation. Agnes the Chambermaid stood to the back of the bed, her hands folded neatly in front of her, her assistants flanking her and wringing their hands. The Head Saint stood at the foot of the bed, mumbling recitations to himself and holding open a holy scripture, an ancient thing with elaborate inscriptions and impressive drawings. A few physicians clustered at the closest side of the bed, conferring with one another in hushed voices.

The room was nearly dark, its corners lost in shadow. The balcony was shut tight against the chill, spring night air. Patches of firelight cast long shadows on the ceiling, on the heavy curtains drawn back to the corners of the bed. Near the knot of physicians, a table brimmed with cups and bottles of liquids, candles, and bowls of burning ashes; the room smelled of singed herbs and tannic concoctions. The table rose out of a pile of cases and tools, glinting metal and glass.

The bed itself was an expanse of layered throws of linen, silk, and fur, the corners and edges dulled into softened mounds that tumbled downward into the dark. Along the side of the bed closest to the door ran a mound of rises and falls, of shadow and highlight, that was The Queen's body. Under the blankets, her form had been wasting away, now pallid skin on a still-imposing form. At the head of the bed, The Queen's face shone pale and wan, encircled by her hair and buried against fluffy pillows covered with silk. She was crownless and in a deep, restful sleep, her lips lightly turned down at the corners.

Kyros approached the King from behind, just as Jaden came to a stop at the bedside. He said very carefully, "W-would you like to see the scrolls, Your Majesty? The p-p-portents for this night?"

"No." Jaden's voice was now subdued, defeated at some level. "Go, as well. It is too late for portents." Then he turned to the physicians and their muttering. "Go! All of you!" A flurry of panicked activity rose while Jaden turned back to The Queen. When it quieted down, Agnes and her assistants too were gone, and all the physicians but one. Jaden turned a cheek to the Head Saint, but kept his gaze on The Queen. "You may go, as well, Saint," he said, softly. There was gratitude and heaviness in his tone. "Have you finished the rites?"

"I have, King. I was just praying."

"Then go pray in the hall, please. Keep a constant vigil there."

The Saint turned to go, and Jaden felt the presence of the physician who had remained, back behind his left elbow. Now Jaden inclined his cheek that way; a flicker of tension in his jaw inviting the physician to speak before he was dealt with more fiercely.

Berenice the Healer took a mouse's step forward and a light breath. "Your Highness? Would you like to know how she is? How long?"

"I suppose so," Jaden breathed out raggedly, gruffly.

"It is our opinion that she has only hours." Berenice phrased each sentence as a question. "She is comfortable, at peace. She will not wake again. We will be ready to administer comforting tonics and to verify the…"

"Yes, Berenice. That is enough." Berenice took three steps backward before turning silently on his heel and leaving.

Jaden stood in silence, looking down at The Queen's face. His gaze followed her hallowed cheeks, her heavy eyelids, and shadowy eye sockets. Her silver hair was still braided but ringed with loose tendrils. The heavy coil of hair snaked down beside her in the bed, ended with a touch on her skeletal hand. Jaden's shoulders slumped forward. He heaved a moan which ended in a cry. He whispered her name, like a plea.

Then he fumbled for her arm, grabbed onto it, and moved down to her hand. He kneaded the fingers, felt like he was going to break something. Jaden had felt clumsy with The Queen's body from the first time. As a younger woman, she could not have been broken, but she felt holy and he like a usurper. She had been the most beautiful woman.

He went down to his knees, bent his head until it was laying on the bed and his forehead was nestled into her side, still warm through the throws. He stayed there for a long time, and when he lifted his head, her hand still in his, he looked across the mound of her at her opposite hand. A flicker of firelight flashed in reflection as it hit the ruby ring, and he squinted in surprise. Then he looked long and hard at the ring.

For all their marriage, he had grave suspicions about that ring. The jealousies that he kept at bay with a king's carousings out of respect for The Queen and his job were twisted somewhere in his stomach. And whenever he noticed the ring, it called to them. Where had that ring come from? Were the rumors to be believed? He had even invited The Angel onto his cabinet, hoping for some sort of catharsis or revelation, but that ended as sudden and anticlimactic as a creek in the woods. Now she would be gone and the ring would endure. She would want him to protect it. Because it was powerful. Because it was historical. Maybe for other reasons. The King shuddered. After all these years, he still quailed at the idea of sharing The Queen's affections with anyone. Yet he knew it had always been part of the deal.

He would bury it with her. She would be covered with jewels when she was buried, as she deserved. And the ring would go with her. Rest in peace.

Then it occurred to Jaden that The Angel might come. Did angels honor the passage from life to death? In fact, would she be going toward him, in a sense? What if he came tonight, came to claim her, once and for all?

Jaden stood. He straightened his shoulders.

"Guard!" he shouted.

One clanked out from invisibility in the darkness of the door.

"Yes sir?"

"Open the balcony door. Make sure it stays open all night, even if it's cold."

"Should we post a guard?" It seemed a silly question, her balcony hundreds of feet from the ground, from the nearest thing, but the guard was spooked.

"Not there, no. No guards in here tonight. Guards in the hall. Once our sons and daughters have seen her, *all* vigils only in the hall, and keep her chambermaids out. Do as I say."

It was eking toward morning when the crowd quieted from a musical hum to individual voices. The entertainers packed up and headed home, except for a lone fiddler who still played one achingly beautiful, melancholy tune after another. Cecily and Conover were left with Daina, Rufus, and their other closest neighbors and kin to batten down the hatches for the night. Cecily stood at the food table, eyeing what was left with much speculation. She yawned and rubbed at her eye.

In the clink of glass and the scraping of wood on wood, Conover came up behind her without her noticing. He very tentatively reached around her waist with his arms. Cecily sunk into his hold, and Conover buried his face in her braids, in the stray hairs, in the bruised flowers and the curve of her neck.

"You have had strong mead?" She stiffened at the smell of it on his breath.

"Yes," he said languorously. "But only a glass. I have never been much of a drinker. Rufus told me I needed some to calm the nerves, make me brave, and I believed him."

She smiled and rubbed at his arms. "You shouldn't believe Rufus." Conover swayed to the music, pulled at Cecily's waist until she joined him, and they danced around slowly—her back to his stomach, him smelling her skin and hair. In the empty space of a vaguely moonlit tent among the demolished grass and the mud, she began learning to relax into the hint of mead on his breath. Conover could be trusted, of this she was implicitly sure.

After a while, his hands had found his way to hers, and he was caressing them as they danced. Then he spun her out, and they were facing each other, their hands linked. She laughed and smiled at him through the dark. "It was a magical day," she said.

"It was a magical day," he agreed. "Just a wedding, but my favorite one ever."

"No, I mean it really was. Could you feel it? As the Storykeeper? This is one of the magic kind of days, the kind stories are made of. There is something in the air." She was whispering now, leaning close to him.

"I suppose." Conover looked around at the few people left, the fiddler wrapping his fiddle in a long piece of linen to carry it home, swaddled like a baby. "But no one talks of such things, anymore. No one believes—"

"I do." Cecily drew close to Conover, looked steadily into his eyes, which were reflecting back small points of distant light. He stared deep into her soul then, reading its subtext for the first time. What he saw there—her tenacious belief in magic, her unchangeable commitment to revere the stories—made him more grateful than he had ever been in his life. And he was more moved, more driven, to lift her up by her waist and carry her all the way from the tent, across the field, over the road, up the walk, and into the cottage. The child was conceived in that very hour.

⌑

All the royal family had been roused from their beds. They

made their way through The Queen's chambers in disheveled robes, hair streaming loose and tears wetting their faces. Nikeas was the most stoic. They found him far from his own chambers, still in his day clothes. Then he stared blankly at the long bulge in his mother's bed, her wrecked visage. Teva put up the greatest fight and was taken screaming and flailing from the room and sedated. She had now returned to the hall, where she paced among the others, a fist mashed against her teary face. The night stretched out past the witching hour.

In the bed chamber, all was quiet. The fire burned low at the grate. It would soon be smoldering, which was the reason Agnes had snuck into the room in the trail of Brando's and Fedel's gowns, past the guards. She sat in the dark, unseen and silent, waiting for the room to chill enough that she would have to stoke the fire and add wood, even if it meant being removed from her lady's vigil. It was almost cold enough.

How could they leave the body alone? Didn't the Head Saint protest? Why didn't Teva break in? Why had the King proclaimed that the night air must be let in? Why were they letting her die cold?

There was a rustle at the curtain beside the balcony door. Agnes strained her eyes at it, could see almost nothing in the dark. A gust of wind moved through the door and picked up the hem of the curtains, ran through the room, and extinguished a few of the candles. In the dark and following calm, Agnes still strained her eyes at the door.

She realized with a leap of the heart that there was an outline there in the balcony doorway.

Agnes dared not move.

The man—if that was what he was—was enormous in physique with a handsome form. He took a step into the room, trailing giant wings behind him. Agnes gasped and then covered her own mouth with her clamped hand. She tried to stop breathing.

The Angel walked straight to the bed but with a gait somewhere between authoritative and tentative. He never removed the tilt of his head from looking at the bed, from The Queen. He came to stand beside her, and in one fluid motion he was down beside the bed, bent at the waist, his torso across the expanse and his arms up. His hands rested one at her shoulder and one on her stomach.

He cried in great heaves but not loudly. The whole bed trembled with it. When he was done, he looked up into her face, then moved more of his body up to where he could cradle her face in his hands, look intently upon her. He kissed her brow, once, tenderly.

Then he stood, and Agnes could see in the small light of the few candles, the starlight, that his grief turned to a smile. He reached out his hand toward The Queen. A pale, multicolored shimmering rose from The Queen's body and suspended there, defining itself. In a moment, The Queen's form, made of a wan light, hovered over her solid body, which had settled downward, almost imperceptibly. The airy form, glistening in the dark, opened its eyes, looked to The Angel, and smiled back as it extended its hand and fitted it into The Angel's.

It stood, or rather it straightened up and floated in a standing position right in the middle of the bed, its thighs disappearing into the bedding. Agnes noticed that The Queen's spirit was no longer weak or emaciated. The form took a step, and it moved forward fluidly, like something more than its steps were propelling it: a wind or a current.

Then the two walked toward the balcony door, through it, and off into the night sky.

The Spring Comes

A bell rang out into the night when The Queen died. For the sad proclamation, they rang just one bell. The largest bell in the bell tower and therefore the lowest tone, it rang a steady, slow monotone. Every morning after, the bell rang again, one hundred times at dawn, the same low, booming peal. It was a long mourning, the ringing of the bells, that went on for more than a month while The Queen lay out in a glass case in a garden of snow. They said she was still beautiful, purified by freezing into a bluish paleness surrounded by the silvery hair. It was a miracle of the ice, and of the long, hard, returned, and lingering winter.

On the first morning with no frost, the body was removed from the garden and prepared for the funeral. That morning, the dawn came with the same hundred notes, followed by a slow, solemn blast of trumpet song from various towers, turrets, and walls of the castle. The mourning dirge had been written by the Royal Musician, and it echoed over the town of Kentwend, bending the ear of all the royals, the courtiers, and the townspeople, who heard it in short blasts with the air currents. They stood at their doors in the receding dark. They were up. They had fed the chickens and washed their faces in icy water. They were ready for the procession.

As the sky lightened, the townspeople lined the town's streets, and the farmers sat down along the roadsides in front of their homes. Shops remained closed, shuttered to the morning air in an official way. Anyone who had mourning to wear or the mourning colors of white or black wore it, as well as a red ribbon or swatch tied around the upper arm. They waited in reverential quiet, shooshing babies, snatching running children from the street to be reprimanded. Their gossip was accomplished in hushed tones.

All kept their eyes on the Branderby Woods, if they could see it, and on the apex of their road if they could not. Just as an orange sun sliced into a placid sky, a carriage pulled by black steeds moved carefully from out of the woods and swung slowly along. The carriage was surrounded by guards and soldiers in black with their scarlet ribbon, hoisting black and white pennants. On the carriage and dressed in white, heaped on all sides by white roses, lay the body of The Queen.

The carriage continued into the farmland, followed by mounted royals and swarms of royal servants and castle dwellers on foot. They made a quiet, slow parade, full of downcast faces. As they made their way through the farmsteads, farmers and peasants cried at the passing of The Queen, sometimes sobbing out loud or emitting a solitary yell, throwing flowers on the carriage and then waiting for the end of the procession where they too could fall in line.

By the time the procession had made its way into the town, it was a snake of people, undulating in and out of roads and byways, sweeping up more townspeople who extended the procession even farther. It continued to work its way along the roads of the Outer Circle and across the Green Moat to the castle's Main Gate and the courtyard. The Queen's body had left the icy garden, had gone once round Kentwend for the people to say goodbye, and was now in deathly state. In a few hours, she would be down on a slab in the catacombs, where only the Head Saint, the acolytes, and the royal family would see her as she was elaborately, methodically shrouded and eventually encased in a niche.

The carriage continued into the Great Hall of the castle, followed by the royals and the prestigious out-of-towners who were allowed to sit. Many who lived in the castle, as well as the forewardmost townspeople who could fit, stood inside. Others crushed into the courtyard or gathered at the Gate, spilling out in a massive crowd onto the Green Moat. Some courtiers returned to their nearby homes to watch from their balconies. The Town Crier positioned himself at a spot above the Main Gate, where he could be heard by the masses as he repeated the ceremony.

Among those standing in a ring against the walls of the Great Hall were the royal employs. Hilary stood with her back flat against the stone wall, shrinking into the vast curtain pulled to the side of one of the archways. She had a straight view to the dais where The Queen was placed, but she could not see much around and over the heads of the others. She felt the urge to extend her fingers and loop them into Meng's, but she stopped at the twitch. Meng was gone.

Hilary imagined Meng, her wrinkled corpse with its long, dark eyes, its gray and black stripes of hair brushed out around her. Meng, as a former concubine of the former king, would have a rather nice burial but nothing as elaborate as this.

The Queen had still been alive at the end of Meng's illness, standing beside Meng's bed as the Head Saint performed Meng's rites. When that was done, even after all those years, Meng asked for a ceremony from her own land, but there had been no one to do it. Now Meng's body was waiting for her turn at a first-thaw burial. Hilary wondered when that would be; after such a long and icy winter, it might take months for the ground to soften and be ready for plowing, for planting, and for burying the winter's dead. Perhaps Meng was being punished by her gods for neglecting her duty at the end. Or perhaps it was The Queen who was punished, denying Meng's final wish while undoubtedly living with the stink of her own hastening death in her perfect, alabaster nostrils.

The room was by now filled with smoke, caught up in the rafters and bluing the shafts of sunlight from the highest windows. It smelled of incense and burning wood. The Head Saint was nearing the conclusion of the ceremony, and the Town Crier's voice rose in the distance echoing off the stone, each turn a little weaker. Hilary felt the person next to her shift his position and clear his throat quietly. She moved her chin just enough to look over at him. It was Lykus the Cupbearer.

As soon as the ceremony ended, the noise in the room rose to a hum of voices while people swarmed the dais, adding a flower or two to the mounds, dabbing at tears with silken cloths. One of the princesses released a moan of a sob that bounced around the room above everyone's heads.

"You're a concubine?" Lykus was looking at her. She was already as far against the corner as was possible.

"Yes." Her molasses hair had been braided for the ceremony into more than a hundred looping strands, tied off with colorful thread down at her chest. In her heart-shaped face, her wide eyes were a shade of blue that was almost purple, her thin, dark eyebrows raised in alarm. She was a distinct beauty, there was no doubt about that.

Lykus's eyes roved around the room in between settling on her face, her squared, slight shoulders, her willowy form in layers of soft, flowing material. No man would want to be accused of ogling one of the concubines. "And you are…?"

"Hilary."

"Ah, the newest."

Hilary shuffled her beaded slippers back an inch. Lykus asked, "Where are you from?"

"The south."

"I suppose I heard that. I've been the Cupbearer a long time. Longer than is expected in my line of work, you know." He smiled at her, not unkindly.

"I know," she squeaked.

"My, child. It will be alright. I'm not going to attack you." He frowned at her a moment, appraised her demeanor, then smiled sadly, again. "Where are your sisters?"

"My sister is dead." She looked down into her open palm, where an apple-colored piece of linen was draped over her thumb and trailing toward the ground. "But the rest of them are here, I suppose."

"Ah, Meng. I see." His eyes dulled into compassion, his hands clasped in front of him and he rocked to his toes. "Well, if you need anything, you can use my name. We are friends. You see?"

Hilary just nodded, tidy little furious movements of the head, staring at Lykus' feet.

◻

The Head Saint turned from the dais where The Queen's body lay as the people started to swarm it. The heavy, silver bowl, overflowing with a slowly rising smoke, swung at the end of its chain in front of his ceremonial robes, the layers of quilting and embroidery making him warm. He took a few steps toward a door at the corner of the Great Hall, followed closely by his attendants.

"Stephyn?" He spoke it out of the corner of his mouth, did not slow his stride or remove his eyes from wandering over the people's faces, blessing them with his gaze.

Stephyn took a couple of large strides, ducking the crowd, until he was flush with the Head Saint. "Yes, sir?"

"I need you to get Herman."

"My brother? Now?"

"Yes, Stephyn. Once The Queen's body has laid in state, we will be attending the burial and cleansing the crypt all night."

"But what about tomorrow…?"

"Bring Herman to the room. Now."

The Head Saint kept his unswerving trajectory, as Stephyn fell back into the movement of the people. Stephyn was surprised, and his gray eyes searched the air without seeing what was around him. Stephyn waited as the Head Saint made his way across the room and slipped through the heavy door at its corner, Stephyn's gray, featureless robe falling stiff to his sandaled feet, his black hair starting to thin at the top and shot through with shining gray.

Stephyn turned then and looked around for Herman. There Herman stood, at the open main door, watching the throngs in the courtyard. Stephyn pushed his way gently toward him and sidled up next to him so that they were shoulder to shoulder in the crowd.

Herman addressed him without turning. "Yes, Stephyn?"

"The Head Saint has asked to see you."

"Now?!"

"Immediately."

Herman sputtered, his helplessness contradicting his strong, soldier's body at salute posture, his soldier's official dress, his stubbled, square jaw, his high forehead which supported a bronze helmet, his spear. "I have duties. Here. It is quite a big day for some of us!"

"For all of us." Stephyn sighed. "You can find a constable to release you, surely. You don't want to ignore the summons of the Head Saint."

Herman cleared his throat. Now he was searching the room for someone, looking panicky. "What does the Head Saint want with *me*?" Then a calm came over his face, mingled with irritation. "Or is it *you*, again?"

Stephyn's voice was metered and calculated. "I imagine he wants to ask you about my long-term accommodations again."

"Stephyn, I'm a *soldier*! I have a family! How can I be expected to——?"

Stephyn interrupted Herman. "Don't ask me these questions again. I have no power to change the answers." When Stephyn caught Herman's eye, his own face softened a bit. "You know I would prefer to stay where I am."

"But there are no grown-up altar boys."

Stephyn sighed. "There are no grown-up acolytes."

"Can't the Head Saint do something else with you? Can't he...?"

Stephyn cleared his throat, lightly, to interrupt Herman. "More things that are not for me to change the outcome."

"Alright, then. I'll look for a man-at-arms." The two turned as one in the direction of the dais, scanning over the heads of the people. Just as they did, a glint caught their eyes and forced them to look at The Queen's body, directly at her hand. A ray of light from a rising sun had slipped through the smoke and settled there. A gleam of red shone from the ring she wore and quickly brightened, throwing red light out in refracted rays around her. A high, single note started so quietly it felt like a vibration in the chest. It rose until it dulled out the crowd's voices—the yelps and screams at the brilliant, ruby light—and the people stood rapt.

The light grew stronger, the note louder, the vibration more pronounced, until a flash of white brilliance shone through the room and the people closed their eyes or shielded their faces. Stephyn stood with his face upturned, his eyes forced shut by the flare of light, but his cheeks, lips, and brow exposed to the wave of warm, scented wind that blew across the crowd and rushed out the doors and windows into the first day of true spring.

◫

It was tradition for some of the royal family to walk through Kentwend in the spring, drinking from each of the public wells. The Head Saint would accompany them, saying prayers of health and prosperity over the water sources. The commoners called it Royal Deluge Day and joked that The Queen had eaten too many pickled things over the winter. It was in the habit of The Queen to perform this rite herself. This year, Teva and Fedel volunteered and dragged along Lulu, Felix, and Osmund. They wore their mourning black, the red bands tied around their forearms.

The week before, Cecily had been weaving in the candlelight, while Conover and Dion drank mulled wine and warmed their feet by the fire. Dion spoke of a young woman who had prophesied at market, telling her cousin and all turned ears that the cousin's child was to be born in the square on Royal Deluge Day and the the baby was going to be a girl. And that girl would marry the next Storykeeper. Cecily hoped with all of her heart that she would be the mother of the next Storykeeper. So she went to market on Royal Deluge Day, looking for the birth of her future daughter-in-law.

Cecily had urged Conover to accompany her.

Conover bent a knee and bowed his head as he approached Fedel in the courtyard. "Your Highness!"

Fedel extended her hand, and Conover pressed his forehead gently to it before looking up again. Teva extended her hand in turn, a smile behind her puffy eyes. "The Storykeeper!"

"Princess Teva," he said simply and bowed again.

Fedel stopped her movement toward the well to address Conover. "How nice that you tell the story of the spring rites of the royals and the wells! Is this a remarkable year for it?"

"It is always wonderful when the first family of Northwyth walks among Kentwend's people. But my wife and I are here today because there is a prophecy that regards us in particular."

"A prophecy fulfilled right here! And today! How marvelous!" Lulu almost clapped her hands together, then remembered the dour affect she must don in mourning. When Fedel gave her a frown, she defended herself. "Oh, but come now! The Queen would love a good prophecy, and you know it!"

Conover stifled a smile.

Just then, there was a cry from across the square. Several people stepped back, making a small clearing around a woman who was bent over on herself, clutching something to her stomach. Then she cried out again, and a younger woman leapt to her side, reaching out to support her. "I told you!" the younger woman said. "You shoulda' stayed home today! She's comin' any moment, and now you're stuck like a pig! I told you!" Her words seemed harsh, but she bustled about, propping and stroking the woman, comforting her.

Others around looked panicked, and as the woman tripped on the hem of her skirt and fell back onto the ground, she threw her arms out to catch herself, and it was obvious: she did not clutch anything *to* her stomach, she clutched her stomach. She was very large with child, and now she was moaning and screaming.

"Let's get you home, cuz." The young woman reached down to help the woman up, but she just shooed her away. "'tis too late," she said through gritted teeth. "She's here." And with one more scream, the courtyard went utterly still and silent.

"What's that?" asked Felix, his eyes wide and directed at the woman. There was a shuffling, and then a muffled screech cut through the silence. It was a baby's cry. And before anyone else could move, the young woman grabbed a blanket from a nearby market stall and threw it over herself and the woman as she sank to her knees. It was like watching two boys wrestle under their bed blankets. In just another moment, the young woman was standing with a giant, brown bundle, a mewling baby face at its center.

"It's a girl!" she called out, tears falling freely down her cheeks.

"Now come! Someone help me get my cousin home!"

Conover met Teva's eye before bustling forward across the square, Cecily in his wake.

¤

Within six weeks of the funeral, more than ten after The Queen's death, the light from the ring had faded, just as the bubbling ripples of blindness had been blinked back and disappeared from before people's eyes. But there was something, something more lasting than the image or the story. People, the town itself, were infected with unexplainable occurrences.

They tried to suppress it. After all, they now had a generation of children who had grown to respect each other's doubt, to erect fences of cynicism over which no questions were asked, no answers expected. Grown men did not literally believe the Northwyth legends. Grown men did not take their old wet nurses seriously when they cackled on about the miraculous end of the War to End All Wars or about seeing The Angel walking the castle garden. When they were kids. Pah! And grown men most certainly did not tell a living soul when they saw flowers floating up from the footsteps of a known prostitute. They did not, when they saw the Candler's twice-aged dog die and come back to life three days later!

But floating flowers and immortal dogs ate at their dreams, and it was changing the town. Perhaps it was changing it back again from something they once knew, like the arc of a circle. Some townspeople were acting like lunatics. Was it rational for John the Son to throw eggs at his own house during vespers and then run through the abbey yelling about stealing from the poor and giving to the rich? Would it make sense for the Sixth Widower to leave his farm, leave his meager holdings, and wander out of Kentwend with naught but his knapsack?

Before long, if the oddness prevailed, the courtiers would be plowing their own lands, the farmers would be dining with the King, and the tradespeople would be swimming in pools of pfennigs! Dion sensed the low hum of disquiet the people seemed to harbor about the turning over of their world, like the groan of a ship changing course.

But what was disturbing—disturbing because it could not be directly ignored or disproved—was a magic, deep magic, calling out from the ground. It called from the crypt, it rumbled silently up the steps, it rattled unheard over the castle grounds, and it permeated the air, the earth, and the water. "Come get me!" it cried. "Come move me, so I can be free to find the other half of the seed. I need to unite the seed!" And it cried in complete silence, but it made arms move and legs bounce and minds reel. The most sensitive of the people, the ones who rode the fine line, they heard without knowing that they heard. And they answered in their way.

¤

Berenice lifted the stick at the end of the rope that tied the gate closed. The rope was worn almost to the point of breaking; the stick could have been pulled apart into slivers and strings it was so old. He moved the gate aside, stepped into the front yard, and closed the gate behind him. He sighed at the state of the farm, at the neglect. And now there were itinerants camped in the adjoining field. This was Daina's Corner, but how was it cousin Daina's any longer? Daina, the Daina who had been the young woman he once loved, had had the life wrung from her long ago, had been bleached into a paleness, a ghost of the girl she once was by the tremoring hand of a worthless husband. He was worse than worthless.

As Berenice walked up the path to the front door, he heard a commotion inside the cottage, and the door heaved open in a wide crack. Daina popped out and shut the door behind her, grasping her shawl around her shoulders. "Berenice!" she smiled through a tired look. "I was just going out to milk Ky." She picked up a chipped earthenware jug from beside the doorframe and gave him her most convincing show of walking off toward the manger.

He walked with her, loosening the tension with his conversation. "I need more Heatheward Extract and more Bubbling Bosmus."

She looked surprised at him. "How many children have had bloodlung this spring? I thought with the passing of winter…"

"The winter cleaned out my supply. More than once, as you know."

Daina approached the cow in her pen. "Yes, well, gentian root doesn't come cheap." She muttered it, a grumble, as she worked herself into a squat for milking.

"That's not your worry. I have it here." He shook the bag over his shoulder, and some items tinkled around inside, and some dry plants crackled.

"What will you pay for my services this time?"

"It's also in there. And the family name."

The milk was now coming in long pulls, making a tinny sound as it hit the bottom of the jug in a rhythm. Daina looked sideways up at Berenice. "Ha! Me make good with the family name!"

"Oh, Daina." His eyes became sad and wistful. His look was intense. "You make good. You're still the best at tinctures and potions." He stood there watching her, and she watched the milk spray, listened to the sound as it turned from tinny to a wet sloshing. Berenice said softly, "You should have married me, Daina."

"Oh, don't I know it, now. Daina the Drunk's Wife. Coulda' been Daina the Healer. Or Daina the Potion Master." She whistled through her teeth. "Ah, water under the bridge."

They stood in this posture not moving, Daina pulling milk, both of them somewhere else in their minds. Berenice jumped at a voice behind him.

"Hello, neighbor." They both turned to see Conover approaching across the yard, a smile on his face and in his eyes, which wrinkled happily at the corners. The effect was offensive to Daina, his being so down-right healthy and cheerful, but she gave him a tolerant look and went back to milking.

"I brought you this." He held out a dense loaf of quick bread, and Berenice took it, smiled a thanks. Conover noticed that he felt uncomfortable but wasn't sure why. "Well, see you later." He turned and loped back toward the gate, just as a few scraggly, red-faced children burst out the front door of Daina's house, screeching into the quiet and running out into the fresh day.

Conover latched the gate behind him and made his way up the road to his own gate, let himself in, and walked up to his own cottage. The door was freshly painted a happy blue, and Conover smiled at that too.

Inside it was subdued, still smelled of baking and was hot from the fire in the hearth. Soon, Cecily would have to move her baking out to the fire pit for the summer. She moved in the shadows under the loft, stocking shelves with food.

"Cecily? I'm back."

"I know. So soon?"

"She had Berenice the Healer over. They were out milking Ky."

"Berenice is her cousin, you know," Cecily called out her conversation to him from her stacking. He removed his boots and came over to the pantry, leaned against the shelf.

"No, I didn't."

"She's a very talented potion maker. She makes some of his elixirs for him and some powders and whatnot. Don't tell, but she does the more challenging work for him." She grimaced down at two plump gourds that would not fit with each other into the spot she had for them.

"I had no idea!"

"Well, now you do. It's a pity..." She didn't say what the pity was. She stopped her organization and walked over to face Conover, her hands on her hips with the fingers around the dent of her lower back. Her hair poked out here and there, flour dusted her cheek, and dough stuck to her apron.

"You look wonderful," Conover said.

"Pfft." She breathed out a little laugh, blowing air at her wisps of loose hair. "Anyhow, I have something I wanted to talk to you about." She looked into his expectant face, forming her thoughts. "I am concerned about all the magic."

He looked curiously at her. "What can I do about that? The Queen dies, the ring goes berserk, people go nutty. There's a story in it, sure..."

"I just want to talk about it is all."

"*Talk* about it?" he said like she had just spoken in a foreign tongue.

"For one thing, I think the royal relics are in danger."

"In danger?"

"Aren't people going to try to steal them? Especially with rumors that the ring is wreaking all the havoc. They say The Queen was buried with the ring still on."

"You want me to talk to King Jaden?" The suggestion was a feeble one.

"And what now of all the magic?"

Conover said, as he often did, "People will have to discover magic for themselves, in the little ways and the small occurrences."

"But they are!" she exclaimed and with excited finality. "They're discovering it, Conover."

"And you want me to——?"

She grimaced at him, narrowed her eyebrows. "Be excited for me? And for you! Aren't people eating up the legends, yet? Turning to them for guidance and legitimacy?" Before he could answer, she continued, whirling back to her previous line of thinking. "I think we should be able to see the ring. To put it on display, as part of our heritage and responsibility. We should remember."

Part of it came down to, Conover knew, job security. He had thought of it too. If the relic was left to molder in the crypt, would the magic wear off and the stories molder with it? Contrariwise, if the ring was respected as a kingdom heirloom, marveled at every day as a stand-in for The Indelible Queen, would it secure his prestige?

Conover bit at his lower lip, looking at Cecily but thinking. "I don't know, Cecily. The King left it with The Queen. I'm sure he has his reasons."

"What if he just *said* so? But really hid the ring elsewhere?"

"Then he has his reasons."

Now it was her turn to look at him and think. Suddenly her serious face flushed. "And I have something else, Conover."

"Yes?"

She searched for the words, started a few times, and then hesitated. "I have missed my cycle for the second month." She let it sink in.

"You mean—?" His eyes widened, the look there an interplay of panic and disbelief and awe. "*Already*?!"

She nodded at him, biting back a spreading smile, and was swept up into a suffocating embrace and danced around the cottage to whoops of joy.

¤

Blaise spat at the earth, turning from the tree and buttoning his trousers. He looked out across the field at the blonde neighbor man with the wispy hair and wiry movements, as the neighbor made his way from Daina's yard back into his own. Daina, now she was a sport. The Storykeeper, Blaise didn't know what to make of him or his cheerful, new wife. Storykeepers were good at seeing through people, seeing what was coming. Blaise kept a wide berth around those types, kept away from the oracles and the fortune-tellers and the magicians, but here was this man living right up on the edge of their encampment. It was dangerous.

Blaise turned his gaze to the edge of the wood in the distance. He scanned the horizon when he needed to think. Sometimes he found movement there, animals or people who didn't want to be seen. That's where he had taken Daina, would take her again, in the shadows of the brush and the bluish trees.

Behind him, the cart began to squeak and tilt from side to side, sending tremors of noise through the hanging pans and other provisions. Musa must be rousing; only women and idiots were still kept in the wagon when the world was warm and their wheels were still. The idiot would sleep until he could smell breakfast. The others were stirring in the tent; Blaise had heard them for the past twenty minutes stretching and flopping onto their backs to look at the tent's top, trying to release themselves from dreams of running without covering any ground.

The door to the wagon opened, and Musa emerged with her mouth already running. "I've got barley here for breakfast. And that syrup you got from Daina." Musa watched Blaise for a reaction, but there was none. "With a little cream, it would be rather nice, but we can't have cream until we have something more to trade with. You getting us pfennigs, yet?"

Blaise continued to watch the horizon and pulled an already-stuffed pipe from his pocket, stuck it between his lips. "Why don't *you* work on that? You have abilities."

Musa lowered her eyes and squatted down next to their fire pit, set the barrel of barley down next to the scrubbed pot and the wooden bucket of rainwater. "I will ask around if I can clean or cook." She spat it out at him.

"You'll do whatever I say." Blaise said it without gall, without even the tone of threat, just as a statement. He would not deign to look at her as he said it. Did he ever look at her, even in the most subservient and defeated of her moments? No. Then he stared at her breasts.

Musa heaved a breath from her chest, as she scooped barley into the pan with a ladle carved from a maple branch. "What about the plan, Blaise? The reason we're here?"

"Don't strain your head thinking about things like that, wench." His look was, again, not threatening, just a matter of business.

"Well, if you ask me, that ring won't be there forever. It's no way we're the only ones with an idea about it."

He ignored her. "Raban still sleeping like a worthless log? Breakfast can wait. Back in the wagon. Come on, now." His eyes were ringed with a puffing pinkness when he turned to look in her direction, and there was a bulge in his pants. He knew that Seti was awake, could hear him. He knew what Musa really was to himself, what she herself would never understand: She was the knife that he could twist at whim to keep Seti in line and, as a bonus, to keep Raban around to be his dumb ox.

¤

When Tarquis strode into town in the dark of a rainy night, he walked straight to the Tavern. He stepped over the threshold into a block of golden light and stood dripping all over the floorboards which were wet already from foot traffic and the occasional gust of wind carrying a cold spit of rain.

Most of the townspeople ignored him, busy leaning forward and gulping at the frothy, sweet mead, leaning back and downing small glasses of liquors of various jewel colors, yelling to their neighbors over the din, over the fiddler and the mouth-harpist in the dusty, dim corner. A few pairs of eyes turned in his direction and settled there, unabashedly following his body from top to bottom. They were unimpressed with his leather knee-boots, his shortpants, his white waistcoat under a heavy coat, his lumpy gunny sack swung over his shoulder, his brimmed hat over a face pocked with brown stubble, cheeks hollowed with hunger, black eyes sunken and sparkling, even the long braid of hair dripping, and the longknife and dagger strapped to his side.

Tarquis surveyed the room and found a seat at the bar, which he occupied quickly. He shoved his sack to his feet and heaved himself onto the stool, sinking into it and slumping over the bar, his elbows on the wood. The bartender stopped turning a pig on a spit over the long, narrow hearth that lined the wall behind the bar. "What will you have?"

"A drink and a meal."

"And what payment will you give?"

"I've got plenty."

"Not by the look of you, you haven't. Unless you mean bedding or weapons."

"I haven't eaten because I've been on the move. And I'm not about to go jangling doubloons around in a strange place." Tarquis cleared his throat.

Theobald, the portly tavern owner with ham hocks for forearms and frizzled hair that ended abruptly at mutton chops, gave him a look of speculation. He seemed like he wanted to believe the stranger but wasn't sure he should. "You've got doubloons to jangle, have you? Well, in that case, hand one over." Tarquis shoved a hand down into a pouch at his waist and came back with a gold coin. His look said, *Satisfied?* and *Now leave me alone.* Theobald snatched at the coin and palmed it as he turned his broad backside and the strained knot of his apron to the stranger. He tore meat from the pig, ladled hodge podge from an enormous, pewter pot, grabbed a roll from a basket, and set it all back in front of Tarquis with a mug of sweet mead. "You have a name besides Out-of-Towner?"

"Mebbe." Tarquis's mouth was already full of bread dipped in thick, rich stew juices.

"In exchange for information then."

It was now Tarquis's turn to assess Theobald for his veracity. He sat still, the smeared bread halfway to his mouth, ogling Theobald with his close-set blue eyes. Then he continued eating. "You can call me Merek."

"In that case, Merek, you ought to know that there is another room to this bar with a door around the back for soldiers only. They take some of their meals there, come for the nightly revels. Always sure to be some around."

Tarquis, his mouth too full to comment, looked up out of the tops of his eyes to meet Theobald's gaze again. Tarquis's look implied nothing more than a reserved thanks.

Then Tarquis ate his meal in silence amidst the yelling, the carousing, the music, the shoving and dancing. While he finished up his third and final roll and his second bowl of hodge podge, Theobald sidled up to him again across the counter.

"You see that man just come in here?"

Tarquis tipped his shoulders and turned his head just enough to see the front door. A small man with straight, sandy hair cut blunt at his forehead, temples, and neck was walking bow-legged to a table across the room. His pasty face, his hooked nose, his bulging, cornflower-blue eyes somehow embodied a look of innocence, even though he clearly seemed to be in possession of the people in the room.

Tarquis turned back to Theobald and gave him his attention while still finishing off the food. "That's Dion. He's the Town Oracle." When Tarquis raised his eyebrows, unimpressed, Theobald hurriedly continued. "Oh, he's real good. There isn't a better. I stay away from 'im in fact. I don't want to know anything I don't want to know." Theobald went back to drying a mug and then filling another and setting it at arm's length down the bar. "Well anyways, you want to know 'im or you don't. Now it's up to you."

Just as Theobald turned to his work, Tarquis grunted, "You got a place I could stay?"

"Sure as I do. There's rooms upstairs, and they're never full. You can have a bed, anyhow. You'll just have to hand over another of them jangling doubloons."

Then the Lost Pirate did what Dion had said all along the lone traveler would do and took a bed at the Kentwend Tavern for the summer.

¤

Stephyn finished up The Queen's daily ceremonies, had the guard release him from the crypt, and left the body out on the stone slab, freshly re-wrapped in oils, perfumes, and clothes. The rites and rituals of the royal dead were long and complicated. It took months for the saints to correctly preserve the body, unwrapping, anointing, and re-wrapping it daily as the skin grew taught and leathery and the purification became perfect; nothing would feast upon The Queen's perfumed flesh. A gloomy light from a distant sun spilled down the stairs and bounced around sparingly on the carved, gray, stone of the floor, ceiling, walls, and cubicles. The wrought-iron gate shut with a loud, shimmying clank and the guard secured it with a solid clunk of the bolt in the lock. Stephyn walked up the hewn stairs into the warm sunshine.

Herman stood ready to meet him. He looked mildly perturbed at having had to wait, but The Queen's ceremonies were as long as The Queen's ceremonies were. Long before, the Head Saint had excused himself for supper and left the final daily duties to Stephyn. What would the Head Saint do without Stephyn? The Head Saint had come into his office when Stephyn was already there, a young man, a novice acolyte able to initiate the Head Saint as much as—or more than—the Head Saint had initiated him.

The one adorned in a gray, wool smock and the other in a soldier's uniform, Herman and Stephyn sauntered side-by-side away from the opening at the wall of the castle, across the lawn, and toward the bridge that would lead the brothers to the Green Moat of Kentwend. The picturesque protection and haunt of courtiers stretched out in front of them. Both walked with their hands clasped behind them, their gait and physique nearly identical despite their striking differences in raiment.

"Are you well, Herman?"

Herman did not answer these well-meaning niceties. Instead, he said, "You must come live with us." He could not look Stephyn in the eye, so it was convenient that they keep walking, slowly, side-by-side.

"Has he given an ultimatum this time?" Stephyn looked tired and disappointed.

"Yes. Sometime after Caominhmas."

"Oh. I suppose I will find some work to do. And I can do women's work."

"My wife has no need of help. The children help." When Stephyn's body went rigid, Herman softened his tone. "I can't help it, Stephyn. It is going to be a struggle. You see?"

"I have always seen." That was why he had fought so tenaciously to be the Old Acolyte, the one and only Old Acolyte. Apparently there would be no Older Acolyte or Elder Acolyte or Immortal Acolyte. He would become the *Old* Acolyte, new inflection, new connotation.

"What else do you propose?"

"You won't like it."

"You mean it is immoral?"

"Perhaps. But it does involve great magic." He risked a sideways glance at Stephyn, whose eyebrows were now raised in curiosity. He put the screw in: "And story. And love."

"What could you *possibly* mean?" Stephyn was amused at these words coming from Herman's mouth.

"There is a royal relic. It is no longer of use. It would be worth a great deal."

"You can't possibly—!"

"I cannot protect the castle and our people, if I cannot feed my own household and give them a roof over their heads." Herman was stern now. With the storms gathering in his eyes, he dared Stephyn to defy him. "It's an idea. And right now, it is our only one. I'll see you at Caominhmas feast. Maybe before then. Get used to the idea, in case I decide we use it." He turned and stalked off back toward the castle, leaving Stephyn to stand gaping at him, stunned and sore at heart.

¤

The Triplets were trying out a new act together. Instead of standing across courtyards or a crossroads and performing solo acts at each corner, they had planned a unified show. In it, each of them took turns as the center of attention while the others assisted. Brom strummed at a lute—and not particularly well—while Bricteva whirled around with her be-ribboned tambourine and a sheer, purple scarf, the bangles at her wrists and the bells on her anklet jangling in rhythm to her melody. Brom fell prey to Butrus's card tricks and appearing and disappearing acts, while Bricteva stood off to the side, her tambourine still in her hand, making expansive gestures with her curved hip and slender, bare arms, and exaggerated faces with her wide smile and heavily lashed lids drawing an "Aw!" or an "Oh!" or a laugh from the audience. Bricteva and Brom dangled from the roof lines of buildings or fell into tubs of water or held venomous scorpions, all in the name of magic. Butrus narrated in a clear, loud tenor while Brom stood bent into extreme, contorted positions, placing his head between his legs to make faces at the audience, bringing one leg straight up above his head while balancing on a sword on a stool.

They even convinced Panther to play along: to call out a question or request from the audience, to heckle, to throw a coin in the painted box, or to draw his bow across a fiddle. He wasn't half bad, but he was incredibly hard to pin down, and outside of practice his participation was unreliable.

Brom's voice rang out across the courtyard, "What would you think to see Brom here sit on his *own shoulders*?" Bricteva stood off to the side, in a position both pointing to the current act and accentuating the way her white tunic fit loosely enough around the neck to expose one nut-brown shoulder and a long line up the nape. Panther was around but unseen.

They had attracted a few children and were hoping for parents to come out of shops looking for their progeny. Instead, a haggard, old woman popped her mole-covered face out of a window above the impromptu performance and yelled, "Enough with the racket! Get your freakish, depraved show off my stoop!" The Triplets could handle all sorts of interruptions and turn it into a show worth seeing, but no sooner had she emerged than the children scattered, terrified. The Triplets packed up sullenly. There was no audience left here, not even for a comic altercation.

Panther appeared in the courtyard, slinking around the corner of a shop kitty-corner to the failed show. He moved along the shop fronts in the shadows of the buildings like fluid human. Brom watched him in the deserted square. Panther sidled up next to Bricteva, and she did not hear him, see him, smell him, or feel him.

"Guess what I heard?"

Bricteva jumped, and Panther grinned a sneering sort of grin down at her, as pleased with himself as he was with her. Even his expressions were fleeting and layered, his voice soft and aqueous.

He waited for all of them to look at him, Butrus still winding a rope around his arm. "The Queen was laid out with her ring. And her body's there in the main room of the crypt. And she's only wrapped in linen. In *linen!*" He jumped forward just a touch at this last revelation. "And I say it's ours! Four ways."

The Triplets looked from Panther to each other, speaking with their eyes.

"Come on! This would be *easy*. Picking the pocket of a *dead person!*" His eyes acquired a manic glint. The Triplets kept looking and coiling rope, not saying anything out loud. "And quit talking to each other in your heads. It's spooky! *And* I know you're doing it, *and* I know what you're saying!" He waited a moment. "All right, then. I'm leaving."

"No, Panther, wait." The fact that it was Bricteva speaking out to stop him sent a flush of tingling through his body. When he looked over at her, she had extended a hand toward him, like she meant to grab him and pull him back. Her hand fell back to her side. "We just keep out of stuff like that, you know. We just open the door for you, and then you do what you do, and the worst that's going to happen is some time in the dungeon. What you're proposing, it's—"

"Suicide," Brom finished for her. "We could be killed for a thing like that."

"Let alone," said Butrus, "cursed for messing with magic that isn't ours."

"You believe that nonsense?" Panther sneered at Butrus, but affectionately.

Butrus straightened his shoulders, stretched out his spine, still coming up a head shorter than Panther. "I do."

"Well, I mean, we exploit the people's perception of magic every day," Brom said.

"No," Butrus turned on his brother. "I *do* believe it. Triplets aren't really magic. What we do isn't magic. But there is magic out there." Both Butrus and Brom turned to Bricteva, looking to her to settle their argument with a vote.

"What I believe," Panther interrupted the spat, "is that I can lift anything and never get caught. And with your powers of distraction and physical prowess, we can come up with something *really good*."

Summer Unfolds

Hilary slipped from her bed early in the morning, before the other sisters arose from their long, languorous rousing, breakfast in bed, and lazing among lace pillows, silken sheets, and perfumed robes.

What was a concubine to do in the morning except rest her long limbs and blather with her sisters in the sun of a long, narrow window with light curtains? What was a concubine to do in the afternoon except lunch with her sisters at a long, lavish banquet table in their own private dining room? What was a concubine to do after lunch except recline on a chaise in the common room, doing needlework and playing a lute or a zither, and gossip with her sisters? What was a concubine to do after leisure except walk the gardens and the Outer Circle green with a chaperone to show off her painted face—behind a mouth veil—and luxurious hair and skin and her royal gifts and garments? What was a concubine to do in the evening except not eat with anxiety, bathe in warm water floating with flower petals, perfume and powder the spots where she could feel a thrum through the skin, and braid her hair? What was a concubine to do at night except wait?

It was enough to make Hilary scream. She soon became known in the Old Harem as She-Who-Disappears, or Umbra.

At dawn, she tip-toed down a less-travelled hall over by the former concubines' quarters, up a narrow passageway, and past the bathing rooms. This hall was always humid in the morning, the bathing attendants heating the day's water and beginning to fill the pools. The passageway ended obscured by an accidental illusion created by a corner and a tapestry of ancient lovers, and it was much cooler and drier as soon as she exited. From there, she wound through the castle, keeping to the secret arteries and walking quickly and quietly.

Out in the gardens the air was sweet and fragrant, each grass blade bent with dew and the trees sparkling in an intense sun. The sky washed from the palest of blue to the pink found inside a seashell. Hilary knew the benches, pergolas, and arbors where she could sit, undetected, for hours and watch as the day unfolded, as the flowers opened their petals and the stalks straightened, unburdened of water droplets. Where did the water go? It did not seem to run down...

When she was, on occasion, discovered, she slid away backward with a bow so quickly that her interrupter could not get in a word of question, reprimand, or greeting before she was just a scent of lavender oil on the garden's breeze. Then she would move back through the passageways to the kitchen quarters, the storehouses, the bakery, and livery and dodge busy workers with questioning glances until she came across Lykus. He would wrap her finery in a plain, brown day-robe that he kept for her. He moved between his chores with Hilary in tow like a father and his curious, little daughter.

They did not talk much. Or rather, they did not talk back and forth much, but often Lykus would explain his daily tasks with a flow of dizzying language. "Over here, see, I am cleaning this out with a squeeze of a lemon and a sea sponge. The lemon is excellent for taking the oil out of the pot, but then we *will* have to oil it again with the cooking oil, so I'm not quite sure why we go about it this way, but that is the way that we do it..."

Hilary blinked at Lykus and watched as he cleaned out the pot, watched as he squeezed the lemon, watched as he brandished the sponge and then scrubbed at the pot, his head disappearing inside with his arms and shoulders. When he emerged, Hilary giggled at the smudge of charred grease on his nose. He flushed and wiped at it with the hem of his kitchen smock. Just to prove his dignity, he said, "I will have to go up to the Royal Dining Hall in a moment, anyhow. It will be time for the King's lunch soon."

She smiled at him and mumbled, "Time to taste the wine."

"That's right, child. And I'm the one to do it." His smile was diffused. After all these years, he was still pensive and nervous as he tested the King's drinks. Or maybe he had only begun again to be thoughtful recently, after leaving this poor, little wren behind. What if he *should* be poisoned? What would happen to her? Well, if he didn't die of poisoning, he would be hanged for his friendship with a concubine.

He knew Meng had been her only friend before. He knew he was her only friend now. He knew the other sisters called her Umbra, and they despised her because she spurned them and dreamt of something outside the Old Harem. It was juvenile, of course, the despising and the dreaming, all of it. She would return to the Old Harem at day's end, just like all of them, and wait, limp and deflated and beautiful and fragile. She would be broken one night at a time, and someday she might even fall in love. This last, he hoped for her.

What she asked was this: "Would you help me escape from here?"

She whispered it, as he was carrying a sack of meal to the storehouses with her trailing closely behind, walking on her toes, her bright, airy fabrics peeking out the bottom of the work robe and at the cuffs. He waited until he had grunted the sack onto its shelf before turning to her, the two of them alone in the dark, dry brown.

"Child, what can you mean?" He whispered now as well.

Her eyes glinted like those of a trapped animal. Was she trapped by her new life or by her vulnerability, now that she had spoken? She said, "I have an idea. All I need is one little thing, and then I will be able to leave here and never return."

"What one thing can hide you, child? Protect you?" He was afraid she thought *he* could hide her and protect her.

Her eyes fell from his and then returned. "The ring, Lykus. The Queen's ring. I have heard wondrous stories about that ring, with the sisters, among the royals in the garden." When he just stared dumb for once, she continued. "It would pay my way anywhere, and with its magic—" She cut off the word by biting at her plump lip with her perfect, tiny teeth. The very word excited her, set her fingers twitching, got her bobbing on her toes, swaying slightly like a reed in a tugging current. She watched Lykus's face for a response. "Lykus?"

He sighed, then looked around the stores as if an answer might be there. "It's just too amazing, child. I mean, it can't be done! To even talk about it—"

"Oh, but I think it can!"

She would believe it. She still had an imagination and her immaturity.

Just then, something clattered at the storehouse door, and Hilary and Lykus turned, alarmed. Lykus moved to inspect with Hilary close behind. Just as Lykus exited the doorway, he caught a glimpse of a cat disappearing fast around the outside corner. He stopped there and sighed. "That was just a cat, but next time it could be a kitchen maid." Hilary leaned out the door's frame, watching the corner, a puzzled look on her face. Lykus said again with a sign, "Next time it could be a kitchen maid," and hoped *that* was the end of *that*.

¤

Nora the Girl Widow wound her way among the people on the Road of Rustics, trying with each sidestep to avoid bumping them and incurring their spite. She imagined herself on her hands and knees, licking a dainty, mud print off of the boot of one of these courtiers, and she smiled to herself. She stopped outside of an imposing residence with a large front window and a few stone steps leading up to the door. Her skirts swooshed and settled. She hesitated, then set her jaw and swept up the stairs.

Aren, Farrah's Lackey, answered the door and motioned for Nora to stand just inside in the narrow hallway. Off to the left, light filtered in from the main room, where Nora could hear voices speaking in hushed tones. Aren walked towards the room with the voices, leaving Nora to stand awkwardly alone and silent. She heard Aren whisper to someone, and the woman's voice ceased for a moment. It must be Farrah the Barren. Would one still call her Farrah the Barren to her face?

Nora listened intently. "You see," Farrah said with a tone of conclusion, "I'm not sure that what you desire *is* a move of household as much as a new employer."

The other voice in the room—a whiny man with a slight stutter—gasped. "That's impossible! I would have to leave t-town! W-we all know that that's what you're doing with Albinus the Third C-c-courtier…"

"Oh, is that his name?" Farrah interrupted, talking to herself.

"...But that is w-*why* I came to you. Impressed by your power! If you c-c-could drive people away, I thought you c-could keep me here and do w-what I ask!"

"You think I'm for hire?" The pause was heavy and brief. "No need to know thyself, I suppose. I will do that for you." There was some quiet movement in the room. "I will think upon it. If I decide I like your proposal, I will come up with a plan. No need to return here; Aren will contact you, or else he will not. Now, good day. I have another appointment waiting in the hallway."

Kyros the Advisor came around the corner and into the shadowy hallway and met Nora's eyes with a residual look of anger and fear. Nora did not know this man, but Kyros assumed he would be known by anyone in Kentwend. What was Farrah thinking, conducting interviews with peasants crouching in the shadows?

He exited, and Farrah called, "Nora the Girl Widow?" Nora hurried into the room and curtsied to Farrah.

"You called for me?"

"Yes." Farrah stood erect, dominating the room, sizing Nora up.

A hardness emerged amid Nora's unsure expression. "I don't like being called for like a dog. And I do mind being appraised with your eyes like a child."

"Well, you are a child, aren't you? The *Girl* Widow."

"Not any longer."

"And you are a feisty one. Aren neglected to tell me of it. That will have to go into consideration." Farrah lifted a long, jeweled hand and placed her index and middle fingers on her lips. "Well, we have what is owed you." She gestured with her hand at Aren, standing at attention in the corner of the room. He had been there, like furniture, holding a tray. He stepped forward with it, until he stood immediately next to Nora.

Nora looked down at the tray top to see a pile of small coins.

She gasped. *How Farrah probably loves to make people gasp, all day long.* Nora had not expected to see any of her payments back, certainly not with the interest promised.

"Take it," Farrah prompted.

"I don't know what to say…" Nora lifted her hands from her sides, hesitating with almost imperceptible jerks every few inches until she had the coins in her hands. Farrah watched as Nora tucked them away in her dress pocket.

"There is no need to thank me or to be surprised. This has been a business transaction."

Nora began a curtsy, but Farrah stopped her with a hand, held up the palm facing outward. "Our business is not done, of course."

Nora's face fell. She was still in mid-curtsy and stiffened upward without completing it.

Farrah said, "We will continue these investments." A pause. "And I will need your assistance in another *small* thing or two." Farrah donned a fake smile meant to reassure Nora. It did not work. "Your late husband was The Queen's Milliner. Is that correct?"

Nora didn't want to answer, her gut dissolving. She wanted to run away, but she saw no other way to answer the patronage, the small favors, the intimidation. "That is correct."

"In that case, you may have some information that I need, regarding one of The Queen's possessions."

¤

Maram and Irene picked their way along the cobblestones of the town on their toes to avoid slick spots and feral cats. They held hands, eyeballed the townspeople who in turn eyeballed them in their fine feathers, flowing, bright colors, and silk slippers with neat, leather undersoles. These were no castle-dwelling errand runners, slipped into rugged, work clothes to run to town. They looked positively out of place. And where were their servants?

Irene tugged at Maram's arm suddenly, and they halted. Maram looked up from the puddled road, shielded her eyes in the glaring sun of midday. Irene pointed. "There!"

Sure enough, a wooden sign hung out a little into the road above a door, reading "Apothecary." They moved quickly, as one body, up to the door and into it, jostling sideways to squeeze the both of them in simultaneously.

It had been hot outside, their hand cloths moist with the sweat they had been dabbing all the way through Kentwend, but it was sweltering inside. There was only a small window to the outside street front, and it was grimed with a salty substance so that it shadowed any filtered light. The stacks, towers, shelves, and tables littering the floor between the four walls of the narrow room necessitated that, even in the day, a few candles be lit. Unbelievably, there was also a small fire crackling in the hearth, and a kettle set over it, bubbling until spittle erupted out the nozzle. Maram and Irene were completely unsure of the smell of the place; whatever it was, it was complex—acrid and sickeningly sweet at the same time.

A stocky man tending the hearth turned around, a spoon and a bottle in his hairy hands. Berenice was dressed oddly in a workman's summer tunic, shortpants, and boots, but with a clean, bright, embroidered hat perched on his neatly curled, brown hair. He smiled kindly, didn't appear to notice their slippers, their feathers, even their clinginess. "Can I help you?" Then he followed their gazes up to his own head, felt there with the back of the hand holding the spoon, and gave a little jump. "My-oh-my! Seems I forgot my castle hat!" He set the spoon and bottle down on the cluttered mantle, carefully wiped his hands on his apron, removed the hat, and hung it on a nearby peg. He reached up and tousled at the curls until they were in disarray. "There. Now, can I help you?"

Maram sighed and jabbed a finger into Irene's side, and Irene leapt forward a step. "Ow! I mean, yes!" She gave Maram a pinched look over her shoulder. "We are in need of a potion."

"Well, I probably have it, but I'm going to need to know *what* potion. Or at least what you need it to do." Berenice smiled again, coaxing his guests and at the same time looking concerned for their recalcitrance.

The ladies looked at each other. They hadn't discussed what to say and found themselves unexpectedly ill-equipped. "Well…" Irene started, and Maram sighed and gave her a reassuring nod as if that were a brilliant beginning. "We need a potion to stay off… that is to say, to keep at bay… well, something *bad*. We've heard you have such things." They both gave him nods at the end, their eyes enlarged and serious. Their arms were still linked but more loosely now.

Berenice cleared his throat and turned around, looking just above eye level at a shelf to the right of the hearth, where dusty books were kept in disarray. "Humph. Let's see," he said to himself. Then he called out to them, "What sort of *bad* are we talking about, here? Animal? Poison? Violence? Magic? Financial? Relational? Political? Judicial?"

Irene's voice came out like a mouse's squeak. "Well… ah… financial, I suppose. And judicial." Then she hastily added, "It's for a friend! And not *this* friend!" She looked to Maram, where Maram was now nodding exuberantly at Irene.

"I see." He pawed through the books and decided on one, pulled it down from the shelf, which sent a few more toppling into its now-vacant place. He thunked it down on a table that was already piled with books and papers and filmed with ash and dust, and opened it up, thumbed through it. Once settled on a page, he moved his thick index finger beneath the words, grabbed a candle and brought it close to the text, and moved his finger along the words again.

"Aha!" he exclaimed, just as a door in the back of the shop swung open, hitting against a shelf of jars and bottles and making a boom with a residual racket of tinkling glass. Maram and Irene startled and screamed. A woman, her arms full of more jars and bottles, entered the room backward, then swung around in constant motion toward a back table.

"Well, Berenice! Look at these two!"

"Daina," Berenice said the way one might warn a child of bad behavior. "Don't pester them. They come looking for help."

Daina smiled tolerantly at Berenice. "Always the soft one, Berny." Then she squatted enough to set all the jars and bottles down and turned around to face the two women, who were watching her along with Berenice across the shop. "And what on earth are you two looking for? Can't be up to any good." Her smile was different from Berny's—calloused, *teasing* them.

Berenice apprehended their wide-eyed stares. "They are having a hard time coming out with it, Daina. I'm sure it's rather sensitive information," respectfully with a raised eyebrow. "At any rate, they came looking for Insulweed Juice."

"Oh, ho!" Daina couldn't help but look slightly pleased at their supposed misfortune. "That *is* something for one of your kind. Well then, Berny, we ought to stock them up." Berenice moved from behind the open book and the table, circled around the room to a shelf behind the ladies, and groped around, moving bottles this way and that and reading labels by lifting them close to his face and squinting.

Daina stood with her hands on her hips, rocking back and forth. She looked from one to the other and back again. "You know, *ladies*, there is word on the streets of Kentwend meant for desperate people to pick up on, so I suppose you two qualify." She waited for them to squirm, then she leaned in and whispered hoarsely, "Someone in need of a gold coin might want to listen *really carefully* to what they're saying, to what's blowing around in the summer wind," Daina wiggled fingers around at eye level for effect, "to the opportunity available to an especially *enterprising* young person. Like yourselves?" Irene looked eminently dubious that *she* was especially enterprising. "Or maybe not. You probably couldn't outsmart all the other thieves, anyhow."

¤

Tarquis couldn't avoid Dion, so he embraced him. Tarquis found Dion an entertaining addition to tavern life—and imagined his insights were invaluable for taking your raincover with you on a Moon's day or for getting an early warning on your impending death. Not that Dion had told anyone of their impending death lately, but Tarquis figured their friendly conversations over lunch were insurance against a surprise in that way.

Dion didn't flatter himself to be very powerful or wise. And he didn't have a problem turning a blind eye to his friends' shortcomings, even if these shortcomings were a dubious profession and suspicious itinerancy. He liked the suave, Secret Pirate. That's why, when Tarquis eventually moved on, Dion gave him the name—Tarquis the Secret Pirate—the name that Conover would use in the stories. At the time though, Tarquis was Merek, the mysterious, close-lipped out-of-towner, transient, and known only to a few as a pirate at all.

Tarquis descended the dusty, shadowy staircase at the back of the tavern and scanned the dim tables for a place to have his supper. Unusually, Dion sat at a table alone, bent over a pot of baked soup and bread—a Kentwend pie. Rose had just topped off Dion's mead, and she blushed as Tarquis slid past her and into the seat across from Dion.

"Any news today?" Tarquis asked, partly in jest.

Dion gave him a wry smile, as he swallowed a hearty bite. "It's going to be hot."

"You're amazing." Day after day had been snaking by in a sequence of scorching heat and brightness. Hot was not news.

"I believe The Sage will surface again." Dion went back to blowing on his steaming pie and stuffing it in his mouth.

"Who?"

It took a minute for Dion to swallow and Tarquis to receive his lunch from Rose. "The Sage. You don't know of 'im?"

Tarquis shook his head, no.

"You know of Northwyth's legends? The Queen and King Jaden and the Demonis? The magic ring?"

"I s'pose, a little." Tarquis gave a half-shrug.

"Well, the stories are very important to Kentwend, at the heart of it all. We have some hundred years of history in those stories. And The Queen is famous. Was famous. In her time, she was a great ruler and also a military leader, and she led Northwyth in the final battles against the Demonis. In her time and in the times before her, The Sage has always been around. He is an advisor, a magician. Some think that he slunk off to die after the war. No one has heard from him for many years. But the Oracle," he winked at Tarquis, "says that he's not dead and won't be dead for a long, long time. He's not like us."

"And he's coming back to town?"

"Yes."

"Why now?" Tarquis didn't have to believe in immortal wisemen to appreciate the information he could find in the details.

"Dunno'. The Queen's death? I wonder if he's coming back for the ring."

"Why didn't he come to The Queen's funeral? Or her death bed?"

"Dunno'. Waylaid? He could probably answer that with some sort of star ascending or something."

"And you think it might be the ring? Is it his, then?"

"Well, no. The Queen got it either from The Angel or the Hag, depending on which version of Conover's story you go with. But the magic came down through the three: the seed, The Sage, and and the stories. I'm sure he's always had his eye on it."

"For what purpose?"

"Someone like Conover would tell you he was out to protect it. Someone less kind might suggest that to bring The Sage and the ring together would create an unassailable power."

"What do you think?"

"I think that The Sage is too smart to want the ring for himself. He's not—well, he's not like that. I think that he wants to lay eyes on the ring and the kingdom, since its caretaker has died. I also think that the ring is now at the center of a vacuum of magical power. The King buried her with it, they say. Now what? It's probably more valuable—in a few ways—than any king's entombed riches."

¤

Outside the castle's Main Hall, a line of commoners threaded through the front door and wove a little ways through the courtyard. Inside, the King sat in state. To the left of the King and a step below on a simpler throne, Brando sat in state as the heir. On a bench off to the side and facing in at an angle, Fedel sat rigid with Felix and Osmund beside her. The boys were there to observe and learn. Fedel was there to keep them in line.

"*I'll* never have to sit in state!" Osmund leaned in and hissed at his mother.

Out of the corner of her mouth, she said almost inaudibly, "When you marry a beautiful, inheriting princess from a neighboring kingdom, you *will*. Maybe you'll marry Enndolynn"

"Blech!" Osmund contorted his face, and his expostulation

reverberated somewhere above a whisper. Fedel shooshed him, and Felix pinched him on the leg. Their grandfather was trying not to look over at the distraction, but the outwardly arched eyebrow warned that he had heard. Osmund shimmied in his seat, straightening his spine and looking positively obedient.

They turned their renewed attention to the proceedings. A middle-aged man was bowing his exit to King Jaden, bustling out backward as he muttered his thanks over and over. A soldier stood at attention at the head of the line of commoners, waiting for the King to address him. "Next!" Jaden said. The voice carried around the Hall with little effort, and the soldier stepped forward, indicating for the next in line to follow him.

He led a peasant girl to the middle of a great expanse of spotless and shining floor. She looked small in the space, and made herself smaller by folding her arms on her chest and bowing her head.

"Your Highness," she squeaked. Then she buckled at the knees. It looked like she had swooned, but she came to rest on her knees and leaned over until her head touched the floor. She let her forehead rest there.

"Please rise, sister." It was a term of affection that the King rarely used in state, but she struck such a piteous posture. Jaden could have been thinking about his own daughters or of Lulu. The peasant girl rose, one knee at a time, and it was evident that it was a great effort. All eyes in the room sized her up—her deeply shadowed collar bones, her too-large eyes, her pale forehead. But she was also a beauty.

She took a breath, and then Felix recognized her as the pretty peasant in the town square. His eyes followed her dress down, and confirmed it: there was the skirt a bit too short, slim ankles, and tiny feet. He wondered what had happened to her. He thought that her face had been burned into his memory, but here she was, skeletal and haunting. The ruddiness of her cheeks had been replaced by an unhealthy flush.

"Your Highness, I am not well." She declined her head again.

"What is it that you need from the King?" Contrition could get obnoxious, and Jaden sounded just a bit testy.

"I would touch the relic." She cleared her voice. "I would like to touch the ring."

In a moment, realization dawned on King Jaden's face, and the room echoed with a drone of murmurs. Felix looked to his father, but Brando was looking intently at Jaden. The King waited for the buzz to settle, while a look of sadness washed down over his forehead to his lips. It was a minute, and the girl shuffled nervously, but her face maintained a look of hope.

"Girl, I cannot. The ring is with The Queen. I cannot—" Jaden's voice broke in a crack that carried into every ear, every corner of the room. Everyone waited.

Another peasant took a step out of line. She yelled, "How dare you?!" The guard moved forward to stop her, but Jaden stayed her with just a gesture.

The peasant girl dropped back to her knees, where she looked from Jaden to Brando to the bench where Fedel, Osmund, and Felix stared back. "I would have touched her robe! But it is too late—" She heaved a dry sob from deep in her chest, then stayed herself. "It was my last hope." She dropped her head and relaxed her posture into a tender S-curve. And there she sat, a sick peasant girl alone in the Great Hall except for her audience of peasants with grievances, the King, and the inheriting Princes.

Felix stood before he realized he was about to. His feet moved him forward, and when he felt the hot gaze of the royal family of Northwyth, he thought he was already committed. He would just help her out, put her hand in his and see her honorably outside the castle. But when he stopped in front of her and offered down his hand, she did not reach up for it. She saw his patterned blue robe in a thick silk. It swished in front of his foot and came to a rest there.

The edging of lynx looked so soft.

She slowly extended her hand forward—the slender white fingers might break if he touched them—and she placed her fingertips on the soft fur. Then there was a sound that Felix thought was a sword being unsheathed, but which no one else heard because of the sharp intake of the peasant girl's breath. Her other arm went convulsively to her stomach, and she doubled over. Her outstretched hand grasped at the robe, grabbed it tight between the sinewy fingers and clean nails.

Then she stopped, as quickly as she had started, and all was silent again. Felix had retracted his hand when she gasped and heaved, but now he extended it again slowly. The girl was staring at the floor, panting. Felix could also tell she was thinking very hard. Then she raised her face and looked into his.

The King leaned forward on his throne. "Are you alright?"

She whispered it. "He healed me."

"What?" said the King.

Felix gave an unintentional shake of his head, but she did not heed it. "He healed me!"

Talk broke out in the room, and several people rushed forward to either drag away or examine the girl. One man yelled, "It's magic!" and before the girl had fully stood, there was an elderly woman laying on the floor before Felix, kissing the hem of his robe.

"No! Please," he begged. He looked from the smiling girl back to Fedel, who was walking briskly toward him, pulling Osmund behind her. Her face reflected his: disbelief and fear.

¤

Lulu sat at the full height of her spine, her mirrors' reflections casting back at her from different angles. She toyed with a small, fluted Egyptian perfume bottle, as Agnes brushed through her long waves of golden hair. Agnes had separated out sections of hair for braiding and looping into the ebony hair piece. Someone knocked gently at Lulu's chamber door. Agnes shifted as if she might go to answer, but the door immediately cracked and pushed open, and Teva floated into the room.

Agnes was disturbed lately by how Teva reminded her of The Queen. She had not the full height of The Queen and not quite the possession either, but in other ways the resemblance was striking. Today, Teva looked tired. It might just be the effect of the mourning black, which was not especially flattering to her fair complexion. Black had never been flattering on The Queen, either. It had been the only color Agnes hated to set out for her.

Lulu looked nice in her mourning black, which was a fact not beyond Agnes's pride. Still, bright colors made them all happy. It would be a while until they were out of black and into whites and grays. It would be almost a year before Teva could wear her sky blue silk, her mossy green, her poppy red. Meanwhile, Agnes was here with Lulu from now until the girl learned some maturity and manners. Years, probably. Agnes supposed that was why she had been given to Lulu: to impart some of her experience with the very royal of royals, the most gracious and graceful of ladies.

Teva nodded to Agnes to acknowledge her and approached Lulu. "Lulu, how are you this morning, dear?" Teva set the tips of her fingers on the edge of the table and looked down at the things on the table top, a sure sign that she had something on her mind. Lulu didn't notice, fiddling with the brush and watching her hair be yanked and twisted into place. If she tilted her chin up and to the right, just so...

"Oh, I'm well, I suppose. I do like it here, really. And now that you have come to visit..." She smiled up at Teva and then noticed the straight line of the lips and the seriousness it implied. Lulu frowned. "Teva? What is the matter?"

"Oh, is it that obvious? I suppose it is. I am always showing my feelings in my demeanor. And this summer, it seems harder than ever to hide… well."

"So what is troubling you, then?"

"It's Nikeas, Lulu."

"Well, he *is* troubling,"—with a light snort out her nose—"I can see your point." She gave Teva a mischievous smile that was returned with a half-hearted one. "Sorry. Go on, then."

"You wouldn't be in the minority to misjudge him. Everyone seems to. But he's really wonderful, when you know him as I do. Wonderful enough, anyhow. I love him, of course. And we have always been the best of friends." She allowed herself a wan glimmer of a smile, her mind clearly tracing over any number of memories that Lulu was not privy to.

Lulu looked not very convinced. "What, then, is *especially* disturbing about my charming uncle, today?"

"Oh, probably nothing. Just my imagination," Teva's gaze flicked over at Agnes as she hesitated, then continued, "I hope, anyhow. You see, I overheard a conversation. It had me up most of the night, replaying it in my mind. *Then* it wreaked havoc in my dreams."

"So, what did he say?" Lulu tried, rather unsuccessfully, not to appear eager for gossip. It was part of her most recent education.

"Let me get this right; I don't want to misquote him. He was speaking to a man when I was about to go into his quarters, and when I heard them, I turned around and left. While I was leaving, I heard Nikeas say that he had the most right to 'the ring' out of any of 'those miserable peasant and courtier wretches' and that he would beat them all to it." Teva went from pensive to wringing her hands and pacing. "Please don't tell him—or anyone!—I have told you this, Lulu. I needed someone to talk to with Mother gone, and normally I would tell Nikeas my worries, but I am awfully afraid of confronting him about this. I don't know why! I *should* ask him about it, and I am sure he would have an explanation for me, a funny story. But that's just it! I am not at all so sure that he *would* have a suitable explanation. He's been so morose lately, so sulky. And he seems to be forever trying to get away from me, to unstick me—" She broke off in a dry sob and buried her face in her hands. Muffled through them, she continued, "Oh, what would Mother think of me now? Where is my composure? My *sense?*"

Lulu stood, pulling her hair from Agnes' busy hands, and smashed Teva into an affectionate embrace. "Teva, Teva, Teva," she cooed, as she stroked her head and her hair. "Sweet Aunt! These are sad times. You have had a shock. And a disappointment. And now to be worried about Nikeas! I think we will throw you into my bed here and cuddle up and demand our favorite, most unforgivable foods and make up what our husbands and our future kingdoms will be like!" She pulled back from Teva and cupped her cousin's chin in her dainty hands.

Teva couldn't help but look into Lulu's big, blue eyes immediately in front of her own, imploring her to cheer up. She laughed, even as she was still biting back a moan. "Lulu. You really are something."

"Something special," Lulu quoted her own mother and winked saucily.

"No argument there."

¤

Rufus worked in the courtyard out back of the bakery while Paccia bartered with customers inside. He was down to his shirt sleeves and shortpants and a skimpy apron and had tied a cloth around his head. Above, another piece of cloth pulled between three poles created a canopy for his workspace to lessen the heat of the sun. Perhaps sweat was a critical ingredient in summer's salt bread? Under the canopy, a large, flat, wooden board stood on stacked bricks near the outdoor hearth. Rufus sprinkled more flour onto his work surface and cracked an egg into the well at the center. Then he mixed with his hands, swirling ingredients into a dough.

He hummed to himself and watched the orange of the egg yolk tint the flour, sensing with his hands and his nose for the right moment to knead. Across the cramped courtyard, an opening led to an alley that ran alongside the shop to the street. A movement distracted Rufus, and he looked up. Kori lumbered awkwardly around the corner, stepping from shadow into the blare of sunlight. It was not a usual type of visit; Kori must have personal business with Rufus for Paccia to send him around back. Then Rufus was further surprised as other men from the Band of Farmers stalked around the corner in single file and filled the small space. The coutyard was too small for six men with the hearth and the table, especially with two men as robust as Rufus and Linos, one of the farmers.

Rufus stopped working the dough.

"Men?" he said.

"Hello, Rufus. You well?"

"Hot!" As he drew an arm across his forehead, his eyes narrowed at the farmers and their muscle. "You?"

"We have some questions for you." Kori could tolerate no more niceties. He cleared his throat before he continued. "You recall what we talked about at Conover the Storykeeper's wedding feast?" Then he cleared his throat several times more while Rufus looked confused.

Rufus said, "I remember. I didn't think you would remember." Manno and Otho laughed gruffly at Rufus's answer. They were both pretty jolly men, but today they stood behind Kori like bodyguards, their hands clasped together at the waist, shoulders thrown back, chins jutted out. No wonder the farmers had chosen this group to represent them to the castle. It made for a pretty successful intimidation. Still, why send the brawn to Rufus?

Laurant, the one with a woman's voice and by far the smallest, piped up, "Can you detail the content of the conversation?"

Rufus looked somber. "No, I can't. I think you might understand."

Laurant continued, "You're afraid *we* don't remember? Why else would we be here, Rufus?"

Rufus remained cordial. "What exactly *are* you here for? To pick my brain? I'll warn you: it ain't much." Manno and Otho laughed again.

"We've come to *include* you, since it seems you know something you shouldn't." He turned to look irritated at Kori. Kori squirmed and cleared his throat again.

Rufus tried to look neutral. He had been thinking about the jewels and treasures buried with The Queen, ever since Kori had slurred some nonsense to him about it at the wedding. But did he want to partner with the Band of Farmers? Could he trust them? Would they be an asset or a danger? He had never imagined this situation in his castle-wandering fantasies, not once.

"You don't really have a choice, Rufus," Laurant helped him. "You already have information, so we need you to take responsibility. And then, of course, there is the matter of reward."

Rufus was still searching for his answer when Linos said in a gravelly bass, "...and the other thieves." Laurant shot Linos a look of disgust.

"What?" Linos shrugged his enormous shoulders at Laurant.

"What do you mean?" Now Rufus was suspicious.

Laurant spoke before Linos could. "We have heard rumors that other townspeople have turned their interest to the crypt, as well,"—and with a wave of the hand—"but those are details we can discuss later."

Linos spoke again, a bit excited. "There's going to be a meeting!"

"A meeting?" Now Rufus narrowed eyebrows at Laurant.

Laurant sighed, summoning patience for his difficult task of herding this group. "Perhaps it's more than a rumor. There is talk of a meeting of the minds: a plan to take the treasure as a group instead of working against one another. The farmers are not yet sure whom to trust. There is much to discuss, but first we must know if you are joining us or working against us."

"Or if you need to be made to forget," Linos added.

¤

There were entrances to the castle besides the Main Bridge to the courtyard and the Great Hall. There were two other bridges, one to the north and one to the south. The one to the north was just wide enough for a horse and cart and was used to stock the larders and bring in linens and other goods, as well as carry away any waste. The bridge ended abruptly at an archway in the castle wall that opened out to the kitchen sheds. It was guarded day and night by soldiers at the archway and lookouts above on the ramparts.

At the south bridge, the wall was thicker and higher and the place more forlorn, less trafficked. At a brambly section of the castle gardens, a tall, wooden door fortified with iron bars opened onto the bridge there. This bridge was also narrow and had been allowed to crumble at the sides so that there was no rail either to the left or to the right to prevent a traveler from falling onto the Green Moat or stepping off into the weeds and bushes that were allowed to proliferate on a sort of ledge along the castle wall. This bridge arched outward toward a crossroads in the Outer Circle, where dirt foot paths led both up and down the Green Moat, and a paved road stretched ahead into the residences of the courtiers. A guard also stood watch at this locked and unused castle door day and night, bored out of his mind.

Furthermore, there was rumor of a secret tunnel into the

castle, meant for the inhabitants' escape in a siege.

When the townspeople started flocking to the castle in search of magic and miracles, they thought only of the Main Bridge and the one that fed the kitchen. Also, amidst the airy homes of the courtiers at the very back of the castle, a small hill with a raised park allowed a curious observer to peek over the back wall of the castle gardens just enough to see the tops of the fruit trees dancing in the breeze. The people crowded the Main Bridge, the northern bridge, and the Outer Circle park, clogging the traffic at all three points and creating a disturbance and a mess.

News of magic and miracles had spread to everyone. That the young heir, the Prince, had healed a beautiful peasant girl caught like wildfire among the frail and poor, the curious and the ambitious. Many claimed to know the source of the sudden spring of magic. They said it was the ring, or they said it was The Queen's spirit. Witnesses said Prince Felix wore the ring when he healed the girl. Others said it was a mere glance from someone of the royal blood that would do it. Fact and fiction tangled and blended. The girl gave birth in the Great Hall. A flash of red seared through the Hall and a song echoed about the place, healing the girl. Hopes added to the stories, and cynicism mangled them. The girl was going to marry the Prince. She was never ill, just a pretender. Worse still, she had been planted by the royals or a power-grabbing, conspiring courtier.

So they gathered. They camped. They stood on tip-toes and invented ways to maneuver closer to the castle. The Great Hall was deluged by a crush of bodies and the desperation of the people who had at once begun to wander up the halls and hide behind the draperies and tapestries, scaring the breath out of Princess Lulu as she walked the corridor to her room after supper. Therefore, the masses were pushed back up the bridges and the Gate locked. They loitered there, on the bridges, and at the park, and they grew and dwindled, depending on the weather and the time of day.

As much as anyone, Cecily was curious about the ring and the magic. Conover was very busy, bustling around Kentwend and the farmlands with the impossible job of untangling the stories to find the true ones, the ones that would be made to endure. He came home one evening and dropped exhausted into his chair beside the hearth. He unburdened his thoughts and struggles over hodge podge, pork, and pickled cabbage set out on a tray. He told Cecily of the crowds, of their unruliness, and of the sad state of some of the most desperate for miracles: the deformed, the elderly, the sick, and the outcast.

The next day, after Conover had slipped out into the still-dark morning, Cecily gathered a few blankets from the trunk beside their bed and filled a basket with bread, meats, and fruit. She hefted the things into the crooks of her arms and shut the house behind her in the lightening of dawn, walking through the dew into town and making her way toward Kentwend's nexus.

There, she found what she expected. The front approach to the castle was blocked by the crowds, many just gathering during the coolest part of the lit day. She turned and walked to the kitchen bridge and found herself part of a throng making its way to fill in the spots left vacant by the night. She kept walking and found herself behind the castle's garden in the Outer Circle park, just a touch higher than the surrounding town. Here, only the groggy campers were still gathered, waiting in day's first blush for the crowds to descend once more. Among the litter and worn-barren ground, the invalids lay abandoned and the children clung, snotty-faced, to their widowed mothers. Cloths had been stretched up to sticks and poles to create a town of random, lonely, squat tents, none higher than Cecily's shoulders. But they were far between, giving the impression that they too, although inhabited, were left like litter.

Cecily made her way among the tents and the bundles of people, offering her blankets and food. She spoke with those there, some of whom she knew or had simply heard of. She asked questions about what they had heard and what they had seen, telling herself that she was contributing to Conover's research. She crouched among the sick, shifting her gaze periodically down at the castle wall, enticing, leafy branches, and the imposing backside of the castle turning gold top-down in the intense, infantile rays of sun. The first stragglers made their way up the hillside with lunches tucked into bundles under their arms and began conversations that seemed to have only just dropped off. Everyone looked toward the castle wall. When voices stopped for a moment, longing and expectation came to the eyes.

It was only the people on the park hill at the back of the castle, only the peppered down-trodden and a few children with Cecily seated among them, who saw what happened next. Up from the garden in a clearing in the trees, a person rose up until his head and shoulders were visible above the wall. Then he kept rising, until his toes hovered above the trees. His eyes were shut, and if Cecily's vision was as good as she thought it was, he was deep in thought and had no idea that he had even left the ground.

A murmur of voices in the park rose to a shout. They were yelling, "It's the ring! The ring has purified the ground around the castle with magic!" And they pressed in, jostling forward toward the walls—the hem of the core of miracles.

◻

The moon, the stars, and the blurry swath of Milky Way were obscured by a thick cover of clouds, although Theobald couldn't see the thick cover of clouds; one couldn't see anything at all on a night like this. Theobald had chosen this night specifically because the Oracle said last week that this week would begin with never-ending clouds and pitch dark nights. It would be better for everyone if the villagers who lived near the Tavern did not notice all the strange visitors Theobald would have this evening. He emptied out and closed down the soldiers' side of the tavern. He waited in the empty room, biting at his nails between swabbing tabletops and the bar top with a greasy rag.

The door swung back, revealing nothing of the dark entryway and the stoop outside the door except a much needed warm breeze. The breeze swept over the tables and over to Theobald, who was staring at the dark space, his rag paused in mid-wipe. A man with salt-and-pepper hair and an acolyte's gray, wool robe led with his head into the room, looking around at the long, empty tables until his gaze settled on Theobald. He looked familiar to Theobald, and when the man was shoved into the space from behind, followed by Herman the Soldier, Theobald knew why he looked familiar: his resemblance to his brother was striking, despite the stark contrast of costume and grooming.

Theobald gave Herman a knowing look and reached around to the shelf behind him for two mugs. "You want mead?"

Herman grumbled a "Yes" and sauntered, muscle-bound and stiff with soldier's thick leather and longsword, up toward the counter. Stephyn didn't answer, although he tried to wave it off, and hung behind until the door swung open again. Stephyn moved to the side as two women entered, looking three times as terrified and out of place as Stephyn, clinging to each other by their thin, fluttering hands.

Theobald ignored them for now. He kept talking to Herman, with whom he was comfortable. "I'm glad you're here first. We should bar the door and have you stand inside, just in case. You can come up with a story to answer any straggling soldiers who might chance by."

"And the door between the front tavern and this?"

"No one ever comes through there, except the ol' ball 'n' chain and the barmaids. It's locked."

"Won't that seem odd?"

"Yes, but it's better than being seen."

Theobald heard the brother in the background introducing himself to the timid courtiers, who seemed eased by having a religious man around. They called themselves Maram and Irene, which, God save 'em, were probably their real names. They were the only two who might not be recognized here, but then maybe he was wrong. Maybe the arrivals would surprise him. Actually, they already had. When Herman noticed Theobald looking at the others' hesitant conversation, Herman piped up. "Stephyn."

"Your brother?"

"Yeah, it's not hard to tell."

"He's in an acolyte's robe."

"Not for much longer." Herman glanced over his shoulder —caught himself. "Well," clearing his throat—"not officially for much longer. I think the weave has bonded to his skin." He cleared his throat again, and the look he leveled at Theobald did not invite more questions, or even laughter.

The Band of Farmers—Kori, Laurent, Linos, Otho, and Manno with Rufus in tow—barged in next. Maram and Irene shrunk a few inches and slithered off across the room, away from the wide, towering men in their canvas and leather, their brown and gray, and their scowls. Theobald wondered if the Farmers had already had a meeting of their own this evening. Why else would they all be crashing in together? Perhaps they wanted others to know they were allied. It hadn't worked immensely well, because the only people there were a couple of shrinking violets, a milksop, and a soldier. And himself. He would know their allegiance, then.

After that, guests arrived more quickly, and Theobald found himself distracted from watching the door and sizing people up by pouring drinks, sloshing mugs, collecting coinage, and writing barters down on his tally parchment.

Once everyone was seated at the longest table, straight down the middle of the room, Herman posted himself at the door. The head seat was vacant for Theobald to settle into. Stephyn sat to Theobald's immediate left, as close to Herman as he could have seated himself with Maram and Irene sitting on the edge of their seats, their drinks untouched, leaning ever so slightly toward Stephyn and avoiding their closest neighbor at the table: Panther. Then came the Triplets: Brom, Butrus, and Bricteva; Blaise, leaning exaggeratedly at Bricteva, and the rest of the Travelers: Drakon, Musa, Seti, and Raban; then Berenice the Healer, Daina his cousin or the Drunk's Wife, and Nora, who was familiar to them only as the Girl Widow. The opposite end of the table, next to Nora, had been curiously draped with linens to claim the chair and the seat across from Nora. After that, Agnes the Chambermaid separated herself with an empty chair from Hilary the Concubine and Lykus the Cupbearer, who seemed awfully chummy. These castle representatives were followed by Hero the Player and the wrongly-named traveler Merek known in the legend as Tarquis the Secret Pirate, before the five farmers and Rufus the Baker. They made quite a party.

Theobald topped off the last drinks, gathered them in his skilled hands, and came around the bar to set them out. He walked heavily to the head of the table, pushed out the chair, and remained standing for what looked to be an opening address. But a knock at the door interrupted him. All fell silent. Theobald nodded to Herman, and Herman unlatched the door, cracked it open, and placed himself as a scrim. After a brief exchange, he stepped back, turned toward the room with a smirk on his face, and made way for an older woman of advanced beauty, who carried herself with more dignity than even her beauty or displayed affluence required. She strutted down the room over the rough-hewn boards directly to the chair at the foot of the table trailing a sheer overdress embroidered with silver seed beads, directly to the chair at the foot of the table. They all listened to the overdress slithering across the floor. A man entered with her and followed. He also had regal bearing, was extremely tall and lanky, and moved around her to pull out her chair as Nora busied herself with removal of the linens. Nora sank back in her chair, her face flushed and her chin lowered into her chest.

Farrah had arrived at that precise moment entirely on purpose. She wanted everyone to watch her arrive, to consider her bearing, her wealth, and her power over underlings. She wanted everything impressive on display: her beauty, her aura of power. Her reputation should precede her, which made it unnecessary for Aren to announce her coming like a herald. In the silence, it was already implied: *Lady of the Underworld, Farrah the Barren!*

She sat rigidly down in her seat and arranged her hands clasped together on the table in front of her. Theobald was about to offer her a drink—which he was certain she would refuse—when another knock came at the door.

This time, the person entered talking loudly, robustly, and Herman looked deeply, deeply concerned as he bolted the door for the last time.

"Ladies and gentlemen!" intoned the youngest son of the great King. "My name is Nikeas and yes, I am the Prince, the son of Jaden. I want to make it known that if any of you should betray my involvement in this meeting or anything that arises from this meeting, I will not hesitate to have you banished from Kentwend or Northwyth—or worse. I have *that much* in my power." He took the seat between Agnes and Hilary, showing no recognition of either of them. Agnes's green pallor deepened, and Lykus sat rooted to the spot only because getting up and running would look worse.

Nikeas too settled at the front edge of his seat, his back rigidly straight and his eyes intensely on Theobald. Theobald was twice ruffled at this point, and he sat down in his chair before calling the meeting to order. He began, "You are all here tonight because you have some interest in what lies in the crypt with The Queen." He gave a look at Nikeas and a *humph*. "If you do not, please stand now, and we will allow you to exit without repercussions." All remained transfixed. If only one had left, there might have been a dam unstopped, but no—they stayed.

As the meeting progressed, each person present glanced around at the other glancing faces, regarding some suspiciously, some with awe or disbelief. Each one's gaze came to linger on Farrah, who was a person of great experience; on the Prince, who was terrifying in his position and highly suspicious; and on Hilary, who was extremely beautiful and completely forbidden to engage.

Theobald coaxed each to disclose who they were and grilled them on their specific interest. Then he had them swear to all present confidentiality and anonymity. He reinforced this point by detailing what sort of things might befall a traitor, but his warnings were nothing compared to the natural consequences that they each felt loomed over betraying Farrah or Nikeas or, for that matter, Stephyn. Some of them sneered to prove they had no scruples. Lykus squeezed the post on the back of Hilary's chair for comfort. Farrah dropped detailed information on the ring from the perspective of the late Milliner, while Nora blushed profusely.

Then, as the hours drained by, they evolved their talk into desires and then plans and eventually the nitty gritty—the things Theobald hadn't been sure they would ever get to. They were an enterprising group of thieves at least, and it seemed that none of them wanted to chance another meeting on another night, or none of them wanted to be the first out of the room, the first to fold out of the inevitable gossip and co-conspiracy. Eyes drooped, courtiers looked longingly at townspeople, who were sprawled with their cheeks propped on fists propped on the table. Linos' stomach made a hungry, grumbling noise. They had gotten to the point in the plan of distracting the southern bridge's night guard.

"He has certain *habits*, certain *appetites*." Herman was trying to be helpful by supplying any information he might have on the man.

Several of the thieve's gazes fell to their laps. Farrah let out a gasp of a groan of a sigh. "Really! There are *ladies* present."

Theobald regarded her with a raised eyebrow, and asked, "Are any of you *ladies* interested in distracting Bernhard?" His voice cracked with use and with exhaustion.

Blaise spoke for the second time since swearing his secrecy. "Musa will do it." Musa was one of those staring at the table directly in front of her chest. Seti grimaced.

"Musa, will you?" Theobald asked, not unkindly.

She nodded and said nothing.

Theobald referred to the parchment in front of him, a long mess of inky blots and squiggles, and croaked a little hum to show he was busy, not nodding off. "I think we have every one on assignment, then. And all the foreseeable problems covered. As we discussed earlier, we will keep communication between us—even siblings," he looked here at the freakish Triplets, suspecting them of already talking telepathically among themselves, "and friends," and he looked at Maram and Irene, who were part of another subset he highly suspected of running their mouths, "to a *bare minimum!*" Theobald raised his voice to make this point clear. "If you don't *have* to talk, *don't.*

"And if you *have* to talk," he referenced the parchment here and raised his eyebrows as he said, "Maram and Irene will handle communications between the castle and the Outer Circle, and the Triplets will handle communications in the town. And the farms? I suppose the Triplets will also handle communication with the farmers."

¤

The alliance between Irene and Tarquis stunk of fear and desperation. Their part in the great scheme was to wait outside the south entrance to the castle with a cart meant for long-distance travel. Together they would take the bag of rice from Lykus—where the ring would be hidden—and drive straight east out of town and then out of Northwyth altogether. Only after they had managed to use Farrah's connections and Tarquis' experience to pawn the ring would Irene have the ability to return to Kentwend and infuse her family's encroaching poverty with life-saving funds. Plus dirt. She figured that all her slumming would amount to enough of it so that she might be able to blackmail the castle, the other courtiers, and maybe even keep the Third Courtier in the Outer Circle. Or dish out retribution before they were driven away with their sack of gold.

But it was not the pale waif with the pale hair and cold expression that drew Tarquis's attention. That honor belonged to Irene's companion, clinging to her elbow. Tarquis—an olive-skinned man himself—was drawn to Maram's waist-length, dark curls and her full, russet lips, her doe's eyes with neatly peaked eyebrows. Whereas a room of thieves and candlelight had made Irene a spectral of ghostly complexion and impassive expression, it gave Maram a flush of red to her cheeks, a darting, daring, alive look to her brown eyes.

Maram feasted off Tarquis's obvious captivation. Along with the narrow, dark room, the heavy smell of peasant, the lewd undertones of conspiratorial conversation, and the bitter mead, Maram had, in a way, actually come alive. Her senses heightened. Her imagination opened. The rules were already broken. So when the meeting was adjourned and drooping eyes traced the wood grain of the floor as the thieves left, Maram and Tarquis made meaningful eyes at one another.

Irene was shrugged off to find her own way home in the deep dark of morning and was understandably offended and terrified. But before Irene could resist Maram's odd behavior, Maram was gone, evaporated into thin air. Irene hurried after Stephyn the Old Acolyte, while Maram stood in shadow around a corner of the alleyway, inches from Tarquis. They stared into each other's eyes, restraining great breaths of excitement while he smirked, a charming, flirtatious smirk that undressed her with its familiarity.

It seemed like he might lean forward at any moment, so Maram sighed and began, "Who are you?"

"Merek. For now." He said it like a question with a shrug.

"Yes, but where are you from? What are you doing here?" When she said *here* it didn't mean just Kentwend, it also meant something like "stabbing your way into my heart and soul?"

He answered in the most obvious way, even though he was assured of his victory by her tone. "I'm a pirate. Or I was, and will be again. I am traveling across land to seek employ in the east. I just happened upon Kentwend in the great kingdom of Northwyth"— said dripping with sarcasm—and yet he said in his eyes that it didn't reflect on her, "on my way through. I found the Tavern. I found Theobald. I found the meeting of thieves." He leaned in so that his breath was hot on her face. "And I found you."

The last phrase, it reminded her of childhood games of hide and seek, but it was so fraught with carnality that it seemed a ludicrous, mental connection. Her breathing had become irregular now, her heart jammed at her ribcage with each bounding thump. But she wasn't done yet, wasn't ripe. She interrupted him, hastily. "You're not staying?"

Tarquis had all night. "Not forever." The word forever would give her enough hope. For him, it evoked a dream of turning this courtier into a woman who would travel with him, would meet him at port after port after strange, distant, romantic port with long, lithe arms open wide to welcome him back to her. She would be a beautiful partner.

She tried out something new. "Well," she sighed and swallowed against her dry throat, "What could make you stay?"

"Now," he adjusted himself so that an arm supported him against the stone wall over her shoulder. "I know you are smarter than that, Maram." When he said her name, it made her startle and her eyes blinked rapidly, looking up into his. "You don't have to play courtier games with me. I already love you."

Now her gaze fell to his lips, then followed his cheek bone down to his jaw, then his chest and the open, top button of his middy with a curl of black hair reaching upward. She snapped her gaze up and spoke louder, crisper. "Well I don't love you! How dare you?" Then she breathed in a whisper, as if it might be the last sound ever to escape her, "I *am* a *courtier*." Her eyes pleaded with him.

¤

Blaise slipped past the Great Hall and wandered the corridors of the castle. Eventually, someone would find him in some off-limits wing, look him up and down, and put him out on his nose. It had happened a few times already since the travelers had arrived in Kentwend. But before he could get much mental mapping done of the east side's upper stories, he turned a corner and found a maidservant approaching a door.

In the first instant, he recoiled, shrinking back to the corner from whence he had come. But with her back to him and a brown curl falling from her bonnet down over her curved neck, he took a step forward. Somewhere between intrigue and lust, he was drawn to this unsuspecting woman in the wide, sumptuous halls of the royals.

She heard his footfall on the carpet, and she turned her back to the door before looking at him. He supposed that had he been a prince or a king, she would stand there, bowed, until he passed. It took only a second for her to realize that he was not, indeed, a prince or a king but a rather rough commoner wandering the depths of the castle.

She hesitated with something on her lips like, "Remove yourself now or I'll call all the King's soldiers on you!" but stopped with a quick intake of breath. Instead, she said, "You!" And when he stood there, puzzling at her and taking in her common, middle-aged face and the brown frizzing of hair around the close forehead, she added, "What do you want with me?"

Then he had it. She was one of the thieves. He sort of remembered her from the meeting, almost entirely eclipsed by all the various beauties in the room: Hilary's brilliance, Farrah's regality, Bricteva's sensuality, Maram's shadows, Irene's coldness. He steadied himself. "Ah. I see. Got a guilty conscience, then?"

Agnes hissed at him, glancing back over her shoulder at the door. "What do you want?"

"I didn't come here for *you*. Everyone's coming to the castle. For magic. For *healing*."—said with a scoff—"For the ring. But no one's come for *you*."

"How dare you insult me!"

"Oh, are you *above* that? I thought you were a common thief." He took a step forward but to the side, as if he were about to slide past her and through the door she was blocking. "Perhaps I should go on in here and have a discussion with—?"

She grabbed his wrist with her hand, circling it with her thumb and middle finger clenching against his skin. Her eyes widened, the blueness flat with fear. She was so close to him, his breath flitted a lock of hair against her brow. "You have no business here."

"How do you know? Perhaps everyone here is part of the intrigue. Even your precious princess." He had said *princess* because he knew she was in service to some royal, and he figured the place was swarming with princesses. The proclamation came off informed and suggestive.

"She would never—"

"What? Betray The Queen? Betray the royal family of Northwyth? So *she's* better than *you*?"

Agnes looked to the ground, and her hand dropped Blaise's wrist. Flatly, she said, "Yes. She *is* better than me."

There was a brief pause for Blaise to notice the shame, and he cried out, "You stupid cow!" He laughed at her behind those icicle eyes. "You really think anyone is better than you? *Everyone's* a thief, woman! Waiting for the next terrible thing to do to get ahead of their neighbor. Forty of us around a table wasn't enough to convince you of that? The prince being there? And three castle employs? Two courtiers? *An acolyte?*" He was so passionate that spittle landed on Agnes, but he was only hissing loud enough for her to hear. She didn't flinch.

"Keep your mouth shut," he said. Then he turned and started back up the hall. Over his shoulder, he said, "Keep your guilt for yourself," and disappeared around the corner.

Agnes stood where she was, her head turned away from the place Blaise had just left. She had grown accustomed to denying her feelings, but her eyes filled with tears before she knew they were coming. She felt a pressure behind her cheeks, and tears dropped down her nose to her chin. She blinked and her eyelashes filled with droplets, turning the light in the hallway diamond-canopied.

She felt that maybe she could stand there forever weeping out her regrets, when a creak alerted her to a presence behind the door. Immediately, it opened, and Teva's voice wafted out before Teva moved through.

She was saying, "Well, I'll see you at dinner, then."

Teva straightened herself away from the door, ready to move down the hall, when she noticed Agnes standing there. Agnes had already lifted the bottom edge of her overdress to wipe at her face. Teva caught her as she was smoothing the wrinkles with the palms of her hands, standing at attention to the princess. "Agnes!" she said, startled. "I didn't see you there!"

Lulu must have been just inside the door, for she peeked around the edge, over Teva's shoulder. "What has happened?"

"Oh, nothing," Teva said. "Agnes must have been coming in and I going out..."

"Oh." Lulu seemed disappointed. But then looking Agnes full in the face, she rushed forward. "Agnes! What has happened? What is the matter?"

Agnes knew she had given herself away with the wetness around her eyes and the flush of her cheeks. And perhaps a faraway, tortured look. It was a very uncommon breach. Lulu took the chambermaid's hands in her own and gushed at her. "Is there something we can do, Agnes? Is it our trouble or yours? I have not offended, have I?"

"No. No, m'lady." Agnes pulled her hands from Lulu's and began again to smooth at her clothing and swipe her fingertips below her eyes. "It is nothing. Really, nothing."

"It's nothing, Lulu. See? She's fine." Teva moved one step away, like she was being drawn backward by a string down the hall. "You sure, Agnes? There is nothing we can do?"

Agnes curtsied. "Of course, Princess."

"I must be going then." Teva took another two steps away and turned halfway between her exit and the conversation. "Lulu? I'll see you at dinner." She gave a strained smile and was off, padding with long, quick strides up and around the corner into another long hall. She thought for a second she saw someone disappearing at the next bend before her, but it might have been a play of the light. Or it might have been Nikeas. She quickened her gait.

For the past half-hour, from Lulu's window, she had seen Nikeas pacing the garden. Perhaps he would be gone before she found him. They had very little time to talk these days. She hardly met with him around the grounds or even at meals. He never came to fetch her from her chambers, and she continually found his empty.

The whip of her skirts nearly tripped her, as she descended a wide set of four stairs which opened up onto a green and a sculpted fountain feeding a pool of bright, Eastern fish. She descended into the garden, and headed straight for a break in the manicured hedge, beyond which she had last seen Nikeas from the bird's-eye view above. She scanned the rose garden as she walked. Then she spotted him, taking a cobbled path up toward the orchard. He disappeared behind a tree, but she dogged him.

The trees in the orchard whispered as the leaves scratched at one another in the heat and dust. It was like they were asking her for help, asking her for a drink. She would have to warn the gardener later. "Nikeas!" she called.

He stopped and turned to greet her, but he did not look pleased. "Dear sister."

"I have been looking for you."

"No doubt you have."

She frowned at the reception. "This is why. Why are you so rude to me? What has happened that you run and hide from your favorite sister? Your closest friend?"

"You're my closest friend?"

The question cut, but Teva wondered if he was hurting her to remain out of reach. "I would like to think so. So why are you pushing me away? Do you have something to hide?"

The look he gave her was worse than his sarcasm. His eyes flashed with fear and what might have been a regret of his previous vulnerabilities. "I have nothing to hide."

"I am unconvinced. And either way, I want to repair what has broken between us."

"You can't, Teva. I've outgrown you."

She sucked in and took a step backward. If he had stabbed her in the stomach, the reaction would have been the same. A light came into her green eyes before they clouded over and flattened.

"Why?" she asked. And he knew she was asking what thing had risen between them, that he would discard her for it.

He turned away from her but stood there, waiting for her to

leave. It was miscalculated, and she stood there too, casting around for something to look at to steady the vertigo of her thoughts. Finally, she said, "Are you in trouble?" Then took a step forward and spoke before he could answer. "I can help you, Nikeas. I will keep your secrets, you know I will."

"No, Teva." He spoke with his back to her.

She flushed and took another step forward. Her next thought made her tremble with anger. "You don't have to protect me, you know. I'll be a queen someday. I have seen things. I know things."

"You're not Lulu?"

"No, I'm not Lulu."

"But you're not mother."

"Maybe I am."

"Maybe not." Then he added, enigmatically, "If I had to choose between the two of you..."

"What do you mean? You're stark raving mad!"

Among the brush ahead of where Nikeas had been looking, a wind picked up and flung the branches into swaying undulations. In a metered moment of clearing, he glimpsed a flash of purple fabric and the unmistakable, widened eyes of Hilary the Concubine. So she was prowling about as well. The castle seemed teeming with scouts and snoops lately. He had sent the Traveler, Blaise, out into the ditch twice already. He had caught Panther shadowing a guard. Theobald beyond his usual circle of the kitchens. Lykus staring distantly down at the entrance to the catacombs. It would be a miracle if the castle did not become so suspicious they doubled the guard. And then how would he get the ring?

He could walk right down to the tomb now, have the guard let him in, and then go out hunting and disappear. Or a hundred other options made straight because he was a prince, the bereaved son of The Queen. The real issue was one of grit. If his mother's heart could not break in heaven, then his sister's certainly would on earth. He had no doubt they would find him out, unless he waited until all the others had played their game. There would be fifty different ways to point his finger then, and pocket the ring and figure out later how much it could do for him.

"Nikeas?"

He finally turned around and saw plainly that Teva had not seen Hilary but was wondering what he was thinking.

"I'm sorry, Teva. I have to go." And with that, he whirled around and disappeared into a hedge.

A Fall Day

$\mathfrak{A}$ren's threats to Nora were vague. He had mentioned in passing an official story about her husband that Nora knew must be either falsified or nonexistent. Then one day, Aren appeared just as randomly as he always seemed to on Nora's doorstep, this time with a strange young woman. The stranger did nothing but stand inside Nora's front door with her hands shoved down into her pocket, when they weren't rubbing at her painfully pockmarked face. Aren, however, went on and on in a dizzying way that left no doubts and yet contained no incriminating moments; this woman was once a little girl who had passed by Nora's window as Nora plotted her husband's murder.

Nora stared aghast at the woman, who refused to meet her gaze.

From that visit on, Aren made it impossible for Nora to wiggle out of the meeting of the thieves at Theobald's Tavern, or for her to gently stop her patronage to Farrah the Barren. And now she had been volunteered to get a key? For a secret entrance to the castle? What did Farrah expect? Magic? Or a miracle? Surely Aren and Farrah were much more capable of getting that key. Was it a test? One that Nora was meant to succeed at, or fail? Either way, it was clear to Nora, if to no one else, that by shunting the task on to her, Aren and Farrah were admitting that they had much bigger chickens to fry than the key they had been assigned to procure.

Nora opened her eyes and focused on the hand-split rafters a few feet from her face and the tiny, paper-thin metallic animals that hung there in the cracks and crevices. She could feel cool air creeping in through the nooks in the wall directly beside her. A thin stream of draft ruffled at a tiny, golden horse. She lay awake for a while. Last night, she had sat up knitting over mulled cider until her last cup had gone stone cold. The scarf for the neighbor's child would have been a better swaddling cloth than a simple neck's protection from another winter's cold. After that, she dreamt of keys and bullies and blackmail and tripped back into consciousness, still plotting with a nervous repetition.

She had no solution for Farrah. She was not the kind of woman with ideas or resources for stealing royal keys.

And underneath it all, she was sure that she didn't want to figure it out, anyhow. Sure, Farrah threatened exposure of supposed murder and the inevitability of falsified justice leading to prison or even death, but all a woman like Farrah could understand was threat as the ultimate motivator. Farrah could not anticipate Nora's dignity, she would not expect it, and Nora knew that in this sense Nora had the upper hand.

It would not be tremendous consolation at the gallows.

Nora could tell by the quality of the sunshine in the window beside the door that it was still early. She had animals to feed and to milk and dough to set out to rise before going into town to sell trinkets at a pittance. She decided not to go sell today, even though it would have been a welcome distraction. She would tend to the animals, do the baking, and visit the doorstep over and over to nervously watch the progression of the sun through the sky.

When she was done bathing herself, dressing, and braiding her hair, the warm from the shaft of sun was combating the cool from the ground, and Nora walked over to the door to open it wide and coax in a breeze. The sun was still low in the sky but rising quickly. When she emerged from the lean-to stable with a pail of milk and a basket of eggs, she looked again toward the sun. It had eked up toward its zenith. She stored the milk, drank a cup despite her twisting stomach, and set neat rounds of dough on the baking board, covered with a damp cloth, to rise. She stood in the doorway then, cooling, noting that the sun was still not at its peak.

Nora was seated on the rock outside the front door over a basket of snapping beans when Aren's shoes and stick-like legs were suddenly before her, a shadow across her tired eyes. He stood almost directly above her, and it was only the northern tendency of a summer sun that let him cast a shadow at all.

When Nora only looked up at him and her body registered no movement upward, Aren was immediately irked.

"You have it with you?"

"No."

"Perhaps we ought to go inside, anyhow." She could tell he wanted to look around at the street and its casual people just then but was purposely staring right at her, like they were old friends and he wasn't the least bit on edge. She also figured he had ways of absorbing what was going on around him without having to turn his face.

"No need."

Aren flushed, and he started to tremble just slightly. Nora had a better view for trembling, down here with Aren's chicken legs in prince's pants. "No need?" His teeth clenched as he hissed it. When she didn't answer, he ventured, "You mean we have to go get it?"

"No."

Now his old cheeks joined in the wobbling. "No?!?" he hissed again, so as not to raise his voice on the street.

Nora stood now, which made her uncomfortably close to Aren on the smallish stone. He refused to budge and she remained where she stood so that her nose was nearly pressed into his chest. She looked up into his eyes but in a way that one would look levelly at someone. "I didn't get it. I didn't even try."

Aren glanced over his shoulder as a nosy neighbor moved onto her toes for a better look at the two of them. Then he recalled his gaze back to Nora and gathered his features into a furious sneer. When he sputtered to begin a sentence, Nora interrupted him.

"Now go. Leave me in peace."

◻

Cecily wondered what the smells and the haze of colorful smoke could mean. For months, the Travelers' wagon had been perched on the hill next to Daina's house. Had the Travelers taught Daina new potions, new tinctures, for Kentwend? Cecily didn't think so. But for weeks Daina's cottage had smelled pungent one day, acrid the next, enveloped in a pinkish smoke on the third. Each day seemed to bring a new aroma, a new texture to the landscape just east of Cecily's cottage. At times, the smells and sights were beguiling, pleasant, even beautiful in the morning mists. At other times Cecily had to don a little wooden implement that Conover had fashioned for the morning sickness. It kept the smells that wafted from the glittering, aqua aura from making Cecily retch, as her stomach grew and grew.

She ran a hand down over her stomach, impossibly round and taut. It wouldn't be long now, just a moon and maybe another half.

Then she lifted her eyes again to Daina's house, where things looked too normal this morning. The air was clear with the promise of a growing heat and smelled only of the sweet grass on the hilltops withering in the last days of a spent summer.

What did she expect? A boom and a puff of smoke and Daina running out on the lawn waving a cat's foot and a stalk of jimmy weed with her hair on fire? What would it tell her, anyhow? Cecily had known for a long time that Daina made potions for her cousin, Berenice. Cecily could even remember back to a time when Daina and Berenice were young and inseparable. Cecily doubted anyone else still remembered.

And yet Cecily stood in the yard and stared over at Daina's, a feeling pricking at her soul.

A distant noise rose to Cecily's ear, and she turned to see two men coming up the road from town on foot. One carried a light sack, the other nothing. She shielded her eyes to see them better and then waddled to the gate to say hello. It was Berenice, who, now she thought about it, had been around nearly every day this week, and Dion the Oracle. Cecily and Dion had been growing in friendship ever since Cecily's marriage to the Storykeeper, and also since Dion had gotten that far-away look in his eyes, had laid a gentle hand on Cecily's still-flat stomach, and announced to everyone in the town square that the next Storykeeper was on his way.

Dion and Cecily had a little club of two that orbited around Conover and took magic in stride. Conover always seemed reluctant to take his place in the magical universe. Cecily and Dion thought it wasn't a far leap from Oracle or Storykeeper to Queen or Sage.

Berenice greeted Cecily first, while Dion grinned in the background, his blonde hair lifting in the warm breeze. "Hello, Cecily," Benerice said as he waved with a thick hand stained with a different color for each finger. He slowed his gait but did not stop as he continued past her gatepost. "I'm off to see Daina, then."

"Good day."

"Good day."

"Good day, Cecily."

"Good day, Dion. Any news?" She gave him a teasing smile. Of course she believed Dion's prophecies, but she still liked to make light of them. It helped that he played along.

His gaze came back less playful this time, and he leveled right into her. "As a matter of fact, there is." He looked up to the house. "Conover here?"

"He'll be returning from town any moment. That is, unless he's been waylaid by storytelling." She said it like his stopping would annoy her, when deep down she was thrilled that more people were asking for stories.

"Perhaps we ought to wait inside? I'll have to leave whether Conover has heard yet or not. Maybe I'll see him on my way back into town? Or you can just tell him."

Dion was not usually a man of superfluous words or of wandering speculation. He rambled until a wrinkle of concern creased Cecily's brow, and she pushed open the gate to him and he stepped aside. They walked the path among the dry, whispering, weedy grasses up to the doorstep and inside. Dion took Conover's chair while Cecily went to boil water for barley tea.

When she returned, Dion was staring, troubled, at the wall. "Dion?" Cecily was hesitant to pull him from his reverie in case it was important.

"Yes. Yes! Well." He wrung his hands as he gathered his thoughts. Cecily forced a cup into his hands and sat opposite him. Dion became absorbed in the steam rising from the cup before continuing. "There is something in the air."

"I knew it!" Cecily mumbled to herself.

"Well... what do you mean?"

"Nothing. Just Daina's house. It's been surrounded by smells and smokes and—well—like an *aura* of something deep and unspeakable." Dion watched her, and when she had delivered her news, Cecily watched his eyes shift around the room as he thought on it.

"Yes. Okay. That might be a part of it. I think your instincts are good. I hadn't known that, about Daina. But then again, there was something about Berenice, a sort of lightning coming off of his skin. Well, not literally, but I think you might know what I mean." He paused for a moment, did more thinking. "Those are only pieces. And, I want you to know, I don't have a clear picture. Not at all. But there are—excuse me—labor pains in Kentwend." Cecily's hand went involuntarily to her stomach, as did Dion's eyes. "I wanted you and the Storykeeper to be warned. To be ready. Perhaps it would be better to say that there is something stirring the water, something moving in the shadows underneath. Yes, that's it. Something is stirring."

Cecily shivered with the analogy, found herself immediately transported in her mind's eye to the side of a large, steely lake, its edges dipping into cliffs and peninsulas. She couldn't see into the water, which was hard in the chill; she could only feel the cool and moisture on her skin, could smell mouldering water plants, could feel a tingle creeping up her spine and notice how close her toes were to the opaque water.

And Dion said something stirred there.

◻

Stephyn became overheated while walking to the castle in the morning, beads of sweat working up under his wool frock. His summer, thinner, wool frock. He descended into the crypt to begin the day's absolutions and offerings, and he knew that later the open air would feel perfectly cool to him, when he emerged from this stuffy heat, from the sacred stench of oils and ointments rubbed into the grave clothes, from the waft of charred grains and meats and singed herbs and pasty incense.

His gaze met with that of the Head Saint, but the Saint closed his eyes and continued quietly to hum and swing the thurible, spreading sweet smoke out from his post at The Queen's head. The smoke sat most heavily over her body, spreading over the white and yellowed linens, hovering about her face, an eyeless, lipless surface with a slight bump where the bony ridge of her nose jutted upward.

Stephyn wished he could strip down to his loin cloth to work in the swelter, like a miner or a housewife in the summer. But the wool frock was holy. Covering his sinewy arms and dripping torso was an act of reverence. Respect.

Grave robbing. Aiding and abetting. Perpetrating. Darkness. Secrecy. Deception. Betrayal.

Stephyn realized that he had been standing dumb and still for too long, that the Head Saint was now studying Stephyn out of the corners of his eyes. Stephyn gave him a weak smile and moved to sweep up the stray crumbs and ashes around the crypt's main room. He worked systematically, pulling first from the far reaches of the space, where it was darkest and the sweeping was done in blindness. Then in neat lines toward the door, carefully nosing the broom's bristles into the cracks and crevices of the space. He worked slowly, deliberately, as all acolytes' work was meant to be done. With rumination and meditation and purpose.

About halfway through his sweep, the Head Saint finished his final morning chant, set the thurible on the implement table, and turned to go. He called quietly and sleepily over his shoulder, "Good day, Stephyn."

Stephyn did not pause in his work but clearly breathed, "Good day, Sir." The Saint shuffled across the room, through the doorway with its grated gate open, and up the stairs into the unrelenting light. His dark vestments were swallowed by the pouring in of sun between the stone walls.

Stephyn kept sweeping. Purpose. Rumination. Meditation. Reverence. Respect. Grave robbing. Aiding and abetting. Perpetrating. Darkness. Secrecy. Deception. Betrayal. As he neared the door, a gust of warm breeze pushed down from the real world and entered the mouth of the crypt, carrying with it a tiny, red leaf from one of the castle garden's trees. Stephyn ceased his rhythmic movement when the leaf came to rest at his feet, the curve of its spine propped against the broom's brush.

Stephyn stared at the leaf, fear building behind his eyes, a panic that had as of yet not overwhelmed him. Then he took some air into his throat and swallowed, continued sweeping, lifting the leaf up one inch at a time toward the exit. Exit. Entrance. In and out. He had chosen the right day after all, the last moment before the world tipped on its axis away from heat and gold, and the Head Saint would announce the Harvest and move The Queen to her forever resting place in the depths of the crypt. In a niche in the wall. Out of the way of prying hands, out of the way of a quick slice of the knife, out of the way of the prying eyes of a man with a simple lantern and a carefully, meditatively, reverentially drawn map of the crypt, of the ritual table, of The Queen's very body and the spot—marked with an X—where her slender hands laid resting under the layers of saturated linens.

He had chosen the right day. Or perhaps not the right day at all.

¤

The Triplets lounged on the thin, stony riverbank that ran under the Maiden's Bridge as it triangulated with a peninsula of the town and then jumped again over the bankless moat into the Outer Circle. There had to be something to water Kentwend, other than the secret, magical spring that bubbled up at the heart of the castle, if that even existed. It was the River Dacidava that nourished them, kept them from evaporating into piles of crackling, sighing bones on the hot days of summer. Or the leftover hot days of pre-harvest fall.

"Damn, this is hot!" Brom said.

"Quit your griping. We're in the shade. And stick your feet in the water!" Bricteva reached down toward her own watery toes and scooped a little, cold water to spatter Brom with a litany of droplets and advice. "Soon you'll be complaining how cold it is and rubbing at your balls to say you'll never be able to have children."

"I never!" Brom complained as he scooted himself up and tested the water with one foot.

"You always," mumbled Butrus, listlessly. "Or maybe that's me."

"Yeah, maybe that's *you*!" Brom still wore offense on his face, heaped up with the further offense of the nipping cool of the lazing river.

"Why do we have to skulk here, anyhow? Why can't we be the ones wandering about on the topside choosing when to grace others with our pretty presence?"

Bricteva bent her body in half, doubling her torso over her bare legs, splashing her hands around by her toes. "I thought you didn't like the sun?"

"But we could just do our business and go home. None of this waiting around and hiding like river rats."

"Oh, shut up and listen, or we'll miss them altogether."

That stopped Brom, and the three of them fell into purposeful silence, listening past the splashing of the river and the echo off the under-bridge, and instead to the rare roll of cart or carriage wheels overhead, the murmur of voices as they carried down from the passersby. It wasn't long before two voices distinguished themselves by moving very close to the railing and projecting out over the view of the river that snaked its way through the town.

The first voice rang clearly into the Triplets' space. "Well, I do hope the *people* are *listening.*"

Bricteva already had a smooth stone sitting cradled in her hoisted skirts, and she picked it up and lobbed it out at the water where it splashed into the river in the sunlight. At that, the voices continued.

"Well, really, I don't know that it even matters today! There is nothing to tell. Simply nothing!"

Brom rolled his eyes at his sister and leaned in to whisper, "All this for *nothing!*"

"Shhhh!" She waved him off and listened, wondering if there was anything more. They couldn't miss anything, not today. And with all the half-speak and veiled meanings...

"No! *Everything* seems to be in *order* in the Outer Circle, *today!*"

What morons. They must rehearse these lines all morning before they come tittering like amateurs over the edge of the bridge. They might as well throw themselves in.

"Perhaps we should go *check* on *our friends*, then?"

Butrus scrambled to stand, startled by the brevity of the day's communication. He was heaving himself up the stones and toward the foot of the bridge to *stumble* into the bridge-talkers and mumble that he had nothing else to add, when one of the ladies up top gave a clipped shriek. Butrus froze and the Triplets listened intently. Then something caught their eyes, something came floating over the edge of the bridge from where the voices had carried. They watched it fall, in and out of the sun and the shadows as it drifted, first white, then gray, then white, then gray, and settled on the surface of the water. They all ogled the hand cloth for a moment before it was caught in the current and sucked downriver. They had seen the familiar scarlet lacing. They knew Maram and Irene were no longer up top.

◻

In the afternoon, Cecily walked to town and around the east side to do some shopping. She was done after the worst heat of the day, when fall revealed itself by early afternoon. She gathered her shawl around her and waddled forward with her basket hung over her arm. Her path carved out into the farmlands, and she cut across the fields to find the road around the north of town. Before it joined Gretl's Way, Cecily stood on the hill, looking down at Daina's Crossing, the Travelers' wagon set back from the road, and her own home in the distance. There was a tree close to the road where she stood, and she sat down below it, still watching the lower hills and valleys, the browning and reddening of the fields and forest, and the Travelers' camp. She pulled a hand pie from her basket, unwrapped it, and ate it, chewing slowly, her brow puckered over an unswerving gaze.

This could not be luck. She watched as a lone figure came from the tent: a man, probably the shifty leader. He met with Daina in the field, and they walked off together across the back of the farm toward the town. Then two more men emerged from the tent, knocked at the wagon, and a man and woman tripped out the door and down the steps. They stood together until they, too, turned and walked up the road in the opposite direction.

Cecily knew there were five travelers in the camp. She could see the Drunk with a horse in the far field, and she spotted a knot of children rushing about, mere dots on the hillsides, threading ever closer to the forest. She crumpled up the wrapping and shoved it into her basket, crammed the last bit of pie into her mouth, and pushed herself up by inches from the ground. Her rounded stomach made everything awkward. Then she wiped her lips with the back of her sleeve and hurried down the hill.

Instead of taking the road, she made a straight line for the

Travelers' camp. She gained speed as she approached, looking around her, checking on the location of anyone she could see. The children were barely visible now, and the Drunk appeared to be lying in the field while the horse grazed.

The Travelers' wagon had a window that faced the side of Cecily's approach. Within several ells of the wagon, Cecily knew the window was well above her head. She looked around at the trash that littered the camp and found a cask. It was empty and light, and she upended it outside the window and, setting down her basket, she climbed onto it. On her toes, she could see inside the wagon. She was not at all sure what she was looking for, but the place was sparse and untidy. There was a narrow bed against the far wall and straw on the floor with rumpled blankets. A long board lined the wall below the window, and Cecily observed half-burnt candles, a lantern, stacked bowls and cups, an open tin of pipe paste, a pack of cards. At the front of the wagon, a bench against the wall. At the back, the door to one side and a shelf to the other, stacked with food stuffs and a few books and papers. At the foot of the shelf, an open trunk spilled with a few bits of clothing.

A distant voice carried to her. "Cecily! Ce-ci-ly!"

She forgot her place and jumped, teetering on the cask before steadying herself and dismounting to the ground. She kicked the cask aside, gathered her basket, and peeped around the side of the wagon toward her house.

"Ce-ci-ly!"

Rufus stood in the thyme, his hands cupped around his mouth, calling to her. He probably thought she was with the cows or chickens. Lazy bones. His back was to her, and she slunk out from behind the wagon and tread quickly and lightly toward her land. But just as she curved around the tent, Rufus turned in her direction for one last look. His face filled with surprise.

He waited until she had come down the hill, past Daina's and behind the stable, before calling to her. "What are you up to, missy?"

"Nothing. I'm just returning from errands."

"You trade with the Travelers?"

"No."

"Then what business do you have with them?"

"Nothing at all. I was coming from town."

"Then why is your face all red?" He smiled slyly.

"The exertion."

Rufus didn't believe this at all, but the idea of the long walk, the goods in her basket, and the stomach protruding before her made his face fall, and he bustled forward. He reached out for the basket and gestured to a tree stump. "Here. Let me take that. Sit. Should you be doing all this? You're going to bring the baby early."

"No, no." She sat down and waved him off, glad that the conversation about the camp was over. "Is there something I can do for you?"

"I brought bread."

Cecily snapped her gaze up into his eyes but worked quickly to look natural. His expression was, behind the calluses, softening.

"Thank you."

He grunted and turned away. "I also have a message from my old lady. She wants you to come to dinner on Sun's Day. You should see the children. It's been a long time." He might have been talking to the grass, but he turned back to her to scowl, "After all, you are their grandmother."

"A strange grandma. About to have a baby, myself."

"Paccia says that familes are made up all different ways."

"My gratitude to Paccia. And we will be there."

◻

Hilary had not been down to visit for a few days. Lykus thought she was being smart, that their not being seen together was in their favor. If accusations ever flew, he could honestly say, "I don't know where Hilary was; I hadn't seen her in days." And vice versa. And any nosy kitchen hand could verify it.

But Lykus also felt lonely and dull. He had looked forward to seeing Hilary come wisping around the outside corner of the kitchen garden, fruitlessly hiding her sheer finery and her startling beauty with a plainer, drabber wrap. He supposed this is what it would be like eventually, when someone in the castle put their thumb down on Hilary: a continual drone of grayer days. A concubine should not be wandering this side of the castle, should not be making friends with the kitchen help, even the Cupbearer. Her friends were in the Old Harem. Her interests were her own pampering, her sisters, embroidery, and serving snacks with dainty gestures.

He felt daunted by her absence. It was harder to continue with the plan without her there. It was all for her, and her beauty and vivacity gave him courage. It looked like he would have to be getting on with his own courage, wherever that was kept. He *was* doing this for her. If it worked out, he would one day smuggle her out of Kentwend and send her on to a simpler, more adventurous life with her stolen freedom and a small nest egg. What price would the ring fetch? And where? Whatever number he came up with, he had a hard time mentally dividing it up by thirty-two. Well, sixteen, because he would give her his share as well.

It was all pretty straightforward, really. Right?

He crossed the kitchen garden with a hasty look at the outside corner of the castle, where there was nothing but the sun and a hot breeze whipping at the withering flowers. He undid the leather thong on the closest supply shed and pushed at the wooden door, letting it creak against the force of his shoulder. It was dark inside and a little stuffy. The area was fairly spacious and the rafters were mostly clean and airy around the hanging legs of cured meat and garlic ropes. The floor of the shed was lined with parallel wooden shelves, heaped with all sorts of sacks and bins of food. The far wall was lined with barrels three high.

Lykus unlatched and shut the bottom half of the door—meant to keep out snooping animals but to let in light—as he navigated the supplies. If he had shut the door and used a candle instead, he would have risked suspicion. He just had to stay alert. Pay attention.

He moved to the furthest corner of the shed, where the light was lost in shadow. He grunted as he shifted a crate on the bottom shelf and then lifted a trap door to reveal a niche between the bottom shelf and the floor. The secret spot had been built into the shelving on purpose, and by the time Lykus had discovered it, it had accumulated an impressive stash of very old wines and liquors, caked thick with dust. They had been forgotten or abandoned, and when he was younger, Lykus had used those that were unspoiled to impress the King and get in his good graces. Since then, he had used the cubby for personal items. It remained his secret alone.

In the dark, various colors glinted at him from the cubby, little pinpoints of reflected light that revealed a substantial stash of potions and tinctures. Lykus had visited Berenice last week, said he was in need of a skin cream, but listened carefully as Berenice instructed him on the uses and proper execution of each sleeping draught. This had to be mixed with that and this combined with this much of that and everyone in the castle would be sleeping early and heavily tonight. They would ask themselves why they yawned so much over dinner. Must be the extra ladle of gravy. Must be the phase of the moon. Must be the unexpected dregs of heat.

Lykus pulled a folded piece of parchment from the front pocket of his work robe. He opened it and smoothed it, holding it up tilted into the dim light. He tinkered around in the glass vials, pulling out one after another that he needed. He used apothecary's spoons and cups to measure out liquids and separate them into different vials, which he stoppered and shifted to his pocket. He was placing everything else neatly back in the cubby when his muted thunking and clunking was interrupted by a voice from directly behind him.

"Lykus."

He jumped from his squat, sloshing a little liquid from one of the decanters, before he looked over his shoulder to give an admonition. "Hilary!" he hissed, but with a tone of affection. "You scared me! I nearly spilled it!"

"You old man," she teased. "I was just having fun."

Lykus closed the lid of the cubby and slid the crate back into place before standing up. "How did you come up behind me so quietly?"

"An old man's ears, that's how."

Lykus smiled at Hilary, who looked back at him in the dark. Her eyes flashed at him, her lips so glossy they reflected the daylight even in the store room. Her teeth glistened as well, like she was made of stars. "I thought you were staying away on purpose."

"I was." She looped her arm into his as they turned to exit the shed. He reflexively unwound his arm from hers. "And now I am *purposely* coming to see you."

"You do everything on purpose, don't you?"

"I don't do anything on anyone else's purpose, if that's what you mean."

Lykus sighed at her as they emerged into the sunlight. He turned to close the shed door while shooing away a cat with his foot and the flap of his free hand. He noted to himself that he should not make too many sudden movements; he was a walking medicine chest.

"So why come now?" he asked her.

"To say goodbye."

◻

Nikeas trembled as he traversed the secret passageways from the royal apartments to the foundations of the castle. The trembling annoyed him immensely. He searched the walls with flat palms, cursed the heat, cursed his cousin Lulu for her habit of waiting around every turn of the passages and Ingrid for following her and Teva for following *her*. Secret passages were meant for dark deeds, not for traipsing girls singing nursery rhymes and pretending to cause some sort of trouble.

He furrowed his brow at the door neatly outlined in front of him. He was at an end. How could he be at an end? It had been a long time since he had used these passages, so he must have taken a wrong turn. It would be better to come out here—in the hallway east of the Great Hall?—and begin all over again with a nearby, sliding bookcase. He pushed through slowly, scanning the hallway through a mere crack before silently emerging with shifting eyes.

He brushed at the front of his vestments and then turned on his heel to the left to make quick work of getting to that bookcase. On his pivot, he froze before he almost ran nose-first into Teva, who was standing there, arms crossed and chin up with fury in her posture.

He exhaled. "Teva!" Then he adopted a more regal tone. "You ought not sneak up on people like that. And look at your face! Anger doesn't suit your features." Did this woman ever stop? Could she not be mortally wounded, like the rest of them?

"I'm a red-head, Nikeas. Red is my color." Her even tones over simmering depths met his.

"Well, good day." He went to push by her, but she moved into his exit.

"What were you doing in that passage?"

"I am on my way to the library."

"For what?"

"A book on animal husbandry. Why—you sound positively suspicious, Teva!"

"To be completely honest, I *am* suspicious of you."

"Teva!" He gave a good show of looking offended. "What could you possibly think I am up to? Meeting chambermaids in the passageways?" *Ooh, that was good.*

Teva's stoniness wavered, but only for a second. Normally she would have threaded her arm into Nikeas' and led him down the hall. Instead, they stood at an impasse. Sure, it was unnerving that Teva continued to dog him and to care about him. But it was worse—far worse—that she had materialized when he was lost, working his way toward the catacombs at exactly the time he thought best for cutting all the thieves off at the ankles. Metaphorically. How could he shake her? Or was this a sign that he should continue to wait and watch? Watch the thieves cut themselves off at the ankles? Metaphorically. He would duck back into the passage as soon as she left...

What was Teva saying? They had started to wander together, and were now looping around the balcony of the Great Hall. Nikeas' attention fell to the floor below, where Kyros, that obnoxious advisor, was shooing off a peasant ruffian, by the looks of him. No, wait, that was Brom, one of the Triplets. "Teva, look," whispered Nikeas. "I don't think they've seen us."

"It was a warning!" Brom hissed his convictions through gritted teeth, leaning in close enough to Kyros that he could smell his breath. It was surprisingly sweet.

"I can't deal in prophesies and portents today, you mule. You aren't even supposed to be here. Those ladies, they are the ones..."

"Don't you hear me?" Brom still hissed his conversation, and he looked over his shoulder toward the door and into the corners of the large, imposing room. He had been here before. The Triplets performed for The Queen and her guests once or twice. Brom had wooed a starry-eyed kitchen girl that night, had had her right in a passageway behind these walls. He didn't think of that now. "Don't you hear me? They are missing! They were on the bridge and then they were gone!"

Kyros finally met the boy's fearful glances, held his eyes there. "Well," he sighed. "Where do you think they have gone?"

"They might have been kidnapped. By Farrah's goons," his voice had dropped to a whisper, "or even the castle guard. Maybe the royals are on to us!"

"Or they might have been spooked. *Perhaps* they thought they were being overheard, so they erred toward caution, not tittering about in large galleries in the castle where they clearly don't belong." Kyros looked upward, searching the balconies now, but Nikeas had already steered Teva away.

"But the hand cloth—! We know. It was a sign that we are going to fail."

"Perhaps you and your freakish sister and brother, yes. But not me. The most recent communication I have received was that everything lies in wait, and today is the day. Now that reminds me, I have work to do. Excuse me." He swished around Brom, across the room, leaving Brom standing there, curled slightly into himself, watching Kyros disappear.

¤

"Well then, Aren," Farrah's voice was very cold. "I suppose that Nora won't be getting our key for us." It took a moment, but then Farrah released into a breathy laugh. Aren joined her in his baritone guffaw until she said, "Enough. It is a loss, even if it is a small one." Aren showed himself mildly chastised. Farrah ran a veiny hand over the bric-a-brac on one of her tables. Her back was to Aren, who stood rigidly to the side of the entryway. "It needn't matter to us." Aren shook his head no. "Let us go, then. There is work to do. We'll get the key, but then we must return to our own affairs."

They walked down the short, shadowy hall, Aren in slight tow, and through the front door out into the insufferable heat and blazing light of a western-dropping sun through a clear sky. Farrah reached into her pocket to remove a tinkling ring of keys and handed it to Aren, who then turned to lock the door with the great sliding of a metal bolt in wooden machinations.

"Farrah." Farrah turned to Aren to listen, her soured face betraying nothing of their friendship to passersby. "I might also mention that Stephyn the Old Acolyte has seen a fallen leaf, which leads him to believe the package will be moved very soon. *And*," before she could interrupt, "Dion is clucking all around the barnyard with feelings of things to come."

"Let him cluck. Let them all cluck." She was about to add something about how they were foxes among chickens, but a shadow slinking along the wide, airy avenue caught her eye. It was Panther the Pickpocket, and he was completely out of place. Farrah followed his movements until she found a soldier, some twenty ells in front of Panther, whom he was resolutely tracking.

When Aren continued, Panther was close to Farrah's porch, and Farrah raised her eyebrows at Aren to stop talking, but for once he did not notice. "Also, Irene and Maram have disappeared." Now *this* was interesting! Farrah watched as Panther heard it, watched as he looked right back into her face and saw how irksome it was to her, then slunk into the shadows of the next house.

The Fall Day Becomes
a Fall Night
or
The Night of One
Hundred Thieves

Stephyn shuddered as he straightened implements on the table near the door of the crypt. The breeze above the surface of the earth had turned colder with the dropping of the sun. He could feel frost on its heels, the hunting horns blowing in the distance, gourd feasts and bonfire revelries. After the long stretch of a drawn-out summer, it would come fast and be short-lived. With the Equinox Festival he would resign his duties as an acolyte.

He steadied his thoughts on the task at hand. Just a little

sweeping of the ashes around the incense burners, and the crypt would be ready for the long, cold night, as quiet and still as the dead. He tried to imagine that tonight was going to be as cold and quiet as any other, that the sacred space wasn't about to be ripped open and desecrated. He hoped, prayed, that Lykus would only cut a thin slice into the carefully prepared fabric, tug at the hand with utmost respect, and disappear into the night like an errant vapor. *What was this thing they were doing?*

Focus. Sweep. Pour the ashes into the bronze bin by the door. Look around the darkness one last time. Back out of the gate, close it. Pat the keys in the pocket, but don't take them out. Lord, don't take them out this time, just let the bolt hang there like a question mark, the fraction of an inch between it and the strike like a great expanse full of electricity and questions, howling at his insides.

It was difficult to turn his body around and mount the steps, but he found himself doing it. He came out into pervasive twilight, the last bleeding of daylight the only thing left to light his way home. Soon the stars would sheath the sky, more distant and pointed on a moonless night, like this one. Anyhow, his work was done. He just had to walk steadily home to the Cloister, and eat his dinner before going to personal prayers. He hoped the other thieves would find their way through the dark, which meant he hoped they might not literally find their way in the dark at all.

¤

Theobald wore his best frock, which was an absurd affectation and not advisably discreet. Anyhow, he did, and no one really noticed it such that they would recall the detail later during the city-wide interrogations. Theobald spent the afternoon on the soldiers' side of the tavern, which was on purpose but absolutely not out of the ordinary. He had come in early in the morning, measured out

Berenice's potions and powders, and mixed them into vats of sweet and bitter meads and into a choice selection of the liquors and wines. He stored them under the bar, lined up at the back behind the day's usual brews.

When the castle's boy came with the cart for the evening's sup, Theobald pulled several of the barrels and bottles from that back row to load. Theobald was always expected at the castle at dinnertime to assist mess for the soldiers, which he did with an especially solemn demeanor. He hesitated to leave the tavern to Rose, afraid she would pull liquor from the far reaches under the bar, but there was nothing to be done about it. Would a soldier even come at mess time tonight? They would likely all be up with him having mead with their dinner.

He walked halfway to the castle and the kitchen entrance, when he noticed the odd looks the people of the Outer Circle were giving him. He stroked at his left mutton chop and looked back at them until he had followed their gaze down to his stomach. He still had his apron on, and out in the fading light of day, it was a mess. No bar or arms of mugs to hide it, no shaded candlelight in the dim of a windowless room. He hastily undid the tie at the back, lifted the top strap over his head, and folded the article haphazardly before draping it over his arm, hugging it close, and continuing. He could feel eyes following him, burning holes in his wide backside.

The kitchen entrance was off around the north side of the castle toward the back. It was accessed by a heavily guarded bridge over a narrow valley in the Green Moat. Theobald felt momentarily relieved to slip into the soldier's mess kitchen through a nondescript door and locate his castle apron on a peg with all the others. He dropped the tavern apron in a heap on the floor and pulled the freshly laundered one up and over his head, tied it with slightly trembling fingers. The vast whiteness felt like absolution.

The feeling didn't last long. He located the barrels he had sent, checked each one for a bronze nail that he had pounded into the edge of each to make no mistakes. He double-checked the liquor bottles, the wine bottles, looking for a small glob of green wax he had sealed onto the tops with a borrowed insignia. He picked at them with a nub of a fingernail in his beefy finger. And when the time came to start serving up drinks with dinner, he directed the kitchen help to the nailed barrels, to the sealed bottles, and served plenty of them himself. He prayed that the heavy drinkers would have no unforeseen side effects. He also wondered which of the kitchen help would get sleepier as the meal wore on.

Several of the soldiers were yawning by the time dinner was over, but Berenice's skill was clear: no one had fallen asleep at the table, and all were strangely subdued. A new moon, perhaps? Theobald watched from the shadows as many of them got up to leave. He would head some of them off on their walk to the tavern. But first his mind flicked to the plan, the great scheme, and the notes he had taken: the parchment he had worn practically into pieces with his perusal of it each night before closing the tavern. He knew it. Some of these wary men would suit up, would disperse through the castle to relieve the day guard, would take their posts at the heights of the castle. There, Linos and Rufus would be waiting for them, walking the walls with Nikeas. They were prepared to deal with any soldier who might see past the drowse and notice anything suspicious in the quiet town below. Theobald could all but see them, standing in front of him, speaking to each other in whispers as they observed the snoring soldiers, the drooping guards. He could feel the cool, night air, could see the breath of the guards as they eyed Nikeas with his companions, wondering.

Theobald left the mess hall and took a dirt path around to the front of the castle, where he could get at the tavern more directly, although not the typical route for a castle employ. The path led up a slope beside the front gate, and he appeared there suddenly, his hands buried under the dirty, wadded apron he carried. He lifted his eyes briefly to see the gate guards, before turning to walk away from the castle, and found Herman already in place. Beside Herman, standing in shadow and sucking at a pipe, stood Blaise.

Blaise was a pawn out of place, but Theobald hurried on.

¤

In the wide, plush hallway outside the royal apartments, by candlelight, Agnes pretended to straighten flowers in a vase on a small table. She was mentally accounting for each prince and princess, as they came yawning around the corner, headed for bed: Lulu and her tutor Ingrid, Teva and Fedel, Felix and Osmund with their chaperone, Jaden with one of the concubines, and now Brando. She would not worry about Nikeas.

Brando cleared his throat as he pulled at the latch on his door. He pushed his shoulder into it and was gone into the warm, firelit emptiness in the space of a breath. Agnes still stood, killing the flowers slowly with her absentminded petting, listening to the sounds coming from the room. If all the others were any indication, the little knocks and creaks would cease quickly.

Lulu had fallen asleep sitting up in her chair, as Agnes brushed her hair out for bed. Agnes had placed her hand under Lulu's arm, whispered for her to "Alleyoop then, princess," and guided her to bed. Lulu's body lay there, thrown on the bed, her face squashed most un-princess-like against the pillows in the candlelight. Ingrid, in the adjoining room, had been snoring.

For weeks, Agnes had been tracking the nocturnal movements of the royals and their house servants. She knew what to expect and when, knew how to rest at the edge of sleep so that small rousings woke her. She wondered how the combination of magic and potions would change things tonight. Where might magic erupt? In the dark, moonless hallway with the ghost of The Queen? Would it be hostile toward the thieves or complimentary?

A chill went up Agnes' spine, and the hairs stood up on her arms. She stopped re-arranging the flowers in the flickering light of the hall sconces. Would the light last the night? She looked down the hall and decided she would spend the watch sitting on a bench in a recess at the turn of the hall. How could she stand to walk the floor, to listen at the doors? The witching hour approached. The cold hand of night squeezed at her heart.

She heard a bang from outside the single window at the opposite end of the hall. She jumped, then she rushed lightly down the hall, listened at the doors as she passed. Nothing stirred. She continued to the window and looked out. In the courtyard, two people skulked about in the cool with bizarre movements, as if they were both compelled forward and alternately drawn to and repelled by each other. She couldn't hear much from the height, but could see by looking down on them that there was a woman and a man trying to be quiet and sneaky but also to hurry. The woman was dressed in fine traveling clothes, and her long, dark hair fell over her shoulders in great waves. The man's clothes were heavily patched, and his swarthiness hid him in the dark. The woman reached out a finely gloved hand, and the man turned and stopped until she had caught up, put her hand in his.

Then they moved out of Agnes' sight into the shadows in an archway against the castle wall. Tarquis yanked at Maram in the dark, pulled her close to him, partly in passion, partly because he was anxious and frustrated. They should be at the wagon already, should be driving to the alley. Irene would be waiting. "Have you ever been in the castle?" Maram's breathing of the question was husky and rattled close to his right temple. New lovers can be aroused by the simplest of things, amazed at their lover's miraculousness when it is really nothing, nothing special at all.

Tarquis, however, was cunning enough to see his own foggy mind and tingling nerves for what they were. "Of course not," he said flatly.

"I forget you haven't been here long." It must seem to her that he had been here forever, right? Always a part of her, or something like that. Destiny. Fate. He could feel the intensity of her gaze at the side of his head as he scanned the courtyard.

No one was there, no one following them. They had a scare and were lucky that Herman had let them duck inside. "We need to go." He turned his face back to hers so that his skin brushed lightly against hers. "You know how to get us to the High Road from here?"

Instead of answering, she kissed him.

Tarquis went cold, pulled back and hissed at her, "Stop that!" and he could see the fire turn to ice in her eyes, to pain and confusion. But he was filling with edginess and righteousness. "Woman! If we don't get to that wagon right now, we are going to blow the whole thing!" Her eyes sparkled with encroaching tears, refracting the light from a tall torch-stand in the courtyard. It only scared him more, did nothing to soften him through his terror. "There's no us without this night! There's no future for us without…"

He sputtered to a pause, and she broke in with a cracking whisper woven with sadness, "We'll make a future!"

"No! We'll take the future now! What do you think? Opportunities to steal royal relics come around every day?" Again, his anger piqued, and he had to take a breath in silence, but Maram said nothing more. "*And have you ever really thought about all this? What do you do with a nearly priceless, famous, magical ring? Do you simply trade it for pfennigs in the next town over? Just waltz up to the first money lender? Or do you just keep it in your pocket and blast holes into walls wherever you go? Take what you want? Make strangers fall in love with you? Make gold levitate into your pockets? And how do you share all this with thirty other thieves?*"

His rage was palpable as a sort of heat, and his whisper-shout had grown loud enough that the last sentence hung in the air at the end, even through Maram's sobs, through her look of fear and distrust. All she squeaked was, "Why now?"

"Why now!" He yelled it, but the phrase soothed him because it made him remember he had to get them both back on track. Calmly, he answered, "Because we're the ones to figure this out. We've got to make the connections with Farrah's contacts in Niska, and Irene is the collateral." He took a step back and ran a hand through his hair. Now his look was apologetic and pleading with a tint of charm. "This is sort of a mess, isn't it?"

Maram took a step toward him and gathered his hands in hers. "It's romantic."

Tarquis thought that was as good an answer as any. He swirled her around to face away from him and whispered into her neck. "Now, show me the way."

◘

Hero stumbled across the bricked road. He careened at a slant with his head tucked down and one arm close to his chest, the other hanging limply so that it wagged with his gait. Only one person walked this bit of the Outer Circle thoroughfare currently. It was the middle of a dark night, and Hero was going to make sure he hit the man squarely without lifting his own gaze from his own feet. *That's the way to do it, old boy! Just barrel into anyone who is out and about. That'll keep 'em distracted.* It was a start.

Just as Hero was about to make contact, the man looked up, startled, and jumped backward. Hero veered with him and swiped him just enough that he could make a show of an excellent fall. As Hero fell, he rolled head over heels. Then he lay there, belly up, kicking his limbs, except for the one arm that was still inexplicably hung limp. He gasped and moaned softly enough that he wouldn't wake the neighbors.

"Well!" the man breathed out, as he watched Hero flopping

about. The man looked offended, but he also looked curious and concerned, which was just the look Hero had been waiting for all night. The last two men Hero had barreled into were impassive and scooted off into the dark before Hero could right himself. *This* was his mark!

So even if no one got hold of that cursed ring, or if one hundred thieves counter-stole it until it disappeared, this would be a performance worth relishing.

Hero flopped and moaned until the man leaned precariously over him, scrutinizing his face. Hero jumped up, almost colliding his skull with the man's. He landed with a physical "Ta-da!" and made one of his eyes rest more than the other. He knew the lazy eye gave him just the look for this job.

"Look, see. All right!" Hero said, brushing off the front of his body. The man looked relieved until Hero continued, "Nothing like a little dip in the river to wash off a day's hard work."

"Pardon me?"

"You know, I've always loved swimming." Hero took a sudden step forward, looping the man's arm into his own, and yanked him into a brisk walk down the street. The man was forced to concede, so they walked together like this through the dark. "Remember when we used to swim in the Dacidava in the summertime? East of the city in that little alcove at the flowery bend with the crooked tree?" Hero feigned a memory and the other man's face fell. Suddenly, Hero jumped away from the man with another flourish of his arms and cried out, "Aah! He's a pickpocket!" And stood, hunched over, looking accusatory and scared, and breathing heavy with his chest and back.

"Well, I—!" the man gasped, then looked over his shoulder where another man and a woman had been drawn from the shadows.

"I never—! I mean—!"

In a flash, Hero straightened up, rigid with his arms crossed over his chest in the position of a mummy. He launched into the singing of a familiar peasant song, during which he responded to no persuasions from the men and the lady to quit. Then, just for extra flourish, Hero yelled out, "This is all, boys! Farewell!" He'd had enough, thought this might just do it, so he crumpled onto himself and fell into a heap at his own feet. He moved no more.

Hero's breath was measured and shallow as he listened to the men and the woman deliberating about him. One of the men prodded at him with a toe before the woman ventured to lift Hero's hat and look into his face. In the end, they decided to use a neighbor's cart to transport Hero to the Head Saint. He thought, *This is exactly it. Yes, exactly.* It was a good long ride around the Outer Circle to the Head Saint, and the procession would be sure to snag up any of the human dregs on the street. Getting the cart, lugging the man, standing around outside the monastery regurgitating the story; it would all chip away at the night and keep the curious from looking up at the castle.

¤

Blaise had grown distant and uninterested in the other Travelers and their affairs. They were aware of it, but they could make neither heads nor tails of it. He wandered far from them all day and ignored them all night. They felt unruddered, for sure. They also felt afraid to make decisions without him. What if he were to return? He would punish free thought or Blaise-less decisions.

Still, they had to meet their assignment for the night of thieves. So, tentatively and meekly, they decided to host a street show, advertised by word of mouth and through the Town Crier. No one cared who produced a street show, so they didn't take any credit, and no one ever asked. They just made sure the whole thing was pulled off. It helped that some of the other thieves were ready-made for a show. The Triplets and Panther didn't really want to be so distracted during the big intrigue, but they were told they could keep the lion's share of any proceeds.

The town's biggest square sat to the south of the Outer Circle's main bridge. Outside of the merry torches and their dancing reflections, it was completely black; light has a way of darkening the world outside of itself. A large crowd gathered, pushing and shoving toward the front of the square, where a stage was set up of barrels, boards, and large swaths of rough, brown fabric. People hollered and laughed gruffly, stepped on each other's toes, and breathed in each other's faces. A pair of musicians—a lutist and a lyrist—played a lively tune at the edge of the crowd, their alms bowls out at their feet.

The Triplets and Panther gathered behind one of the curtains. Bricteva trembled her hands with an imaginary tambourine and swirled her hips repetitively in an asymmetric movement. Brom doubled over on himself, wove his arms with his ankles, and stretched. Butrus shoved a piece of colorful fabric up his shirt sleeve and smoothed it over. Panther alone seemed mentally absent, bounced on the balls of his feet as he glanced compulsively to the right and the left and then back at Bricteva and her sashaying.

Panther's gaze fell out on the surge of crowd that spilled back behind the stage around to the street side. Then it shifted to Bricteva, then back to the crowd, then over to the other side of the curtain, where the Travelers stood looking like they were neither spectator nor performer. Seti and Drakon had turned in on each other, exchanging knowing looks, while Raban watched the crowd himself, bouncing at the knees, giggling at the commotion.

"*Where is he?*" Drakon spat out a whisper, his eyebrows knit in anger.

"He's not here." Seti shrugged it off, not entirely convincing.

"I *know* he's not here. Where is he?"

"You think I know?" Seti laughed at this, a low emission of

air and a scoff.

Drakon mumbled, "No, I don't suppose you would." Seti knew what he was implying, what he was thinking. If anyone had known of Blaise's plans, it would be Drakon first. If Drakon didn't know, then they were all in the dark.

◻

The night's brosh had reduced to a syrupy, charred mess in the bottom of the kettle by the time Conover came home. Cecily sat on a wooden chair at the hearth side, weaving distractedly at something that no longer resembled a baby swaddling. Her increasing weight stressed the stool, and it creaked whenever she adjusted, trying unsuccessfully to get comfortable around her enormous belly, the pull of it against her pelvis and thighs, the looseness in the joints of her hands, and the thickness of her ankles and feet straining against the leather of her shoes.

As soon as Conover touched his hand to the latch at the door, Cecily's eyes were up and trained on it. When he stepped in, her look was wild upon him. He looked away and closed the door behind him.

"Conover!" She hoped that he could stop the fire in her heart with a magical explanation.

"Cecily? Are you all right?"

This was not the proper incantation. "No, I'm not all right. I was scared you were eaten by a wolf, the dinner is ruined, and I've had something important to say to you all day. I sincerely hope you met Dion on the road, somewhere?"

"I—"

"Speaking of which, where were you all day?"

"I—"

"Nevermind. I've been stewing in my juices, worried and

uncomfortable and helpless."

"Worried? Uncomfortable? Helpless?" Each word brought a little more distress into Conover's voice. "Why were you——?"

"Dion came to see us this afternoon. He wanted to speak to you, but he had to leave the message with me in case he couldn't find you. Did he not find you?" Her hands stopped off weaving, and she flopped them down where they grasped her stomach. She looked with a tilted head at her befuddled husband.

"No, he didn't."

"Can you not feel the magic *at all* anymore?"

He finally took a couple strides toward her across the floor. "Cecily, I don't know what you mean."

She looked on him with pity, a look Conover did not enjoy. "Dion says that there is something happening. I can feel it. For heaven's sake, the child inside me can feel it. He's been kicking at my heart all day, kneading his knees and knuckles into my insides, trying to get out." Her hands rubbed at her stomach, the loom just getting in the way as she bumped her knuckles against it. Conover took his last step forward, reached out, and gently took her hands and turned her body away from the loom, toward the room, toward him.

He crouched in front of her and looked her in the face. His voice was soothing: "Cecily, I'm just the Story*keeper*. I'm not even sure if interfering is appropriate."

"Appropriate?" Her eyes went terribly wide. "What about *right*?"

"It's just a ring, Cecily."

"Just a ring?"

"And if it is magic, which I *do* believe,"—he was only partly convincing—"then it will take care of itself. Everything will resolve itself eventually." Of that, he was fully convinced.

Cecily sat very still, staring at Conover, who also remained still and squatting, until she said, "Let me ask you something. Why do you think I can feel magic?"

She could tell he was afraid to answer her and offend her, but she waited. "I don't know." That wasn't enough. "It's a gift?"

"But a gift, *why*?"

"Clearly you believe it's for me to go traipsing off into the dark night to slink around the castle like a common thief waiting for a thug to jump out and kill me."

"No, I see that isn't so." She stood up with effort, and he did too. A redness flushed into her face and some hair fell from under her cap. "It's for *me* to go traipsing off into the night to slink around the castle like a common thief. God save you if I'm killed with the baby!" She was already bustling and waddling around the room, gathering her cloak.

"Now, you know I would never let you do that." He didn't say it as a command but with a great deal of concern.

Just then, Cecily dropped her cloak and grabbed at her lower back, sucked in a large breath of air. Conover rushed to her and was herding her back toward the chair when she started to breathe again. "God Almighty! Child, calm down!" Then to Conover, "I've been telling him to calm all day, but the pain keeps coming back, the squeezing." He could tell she was doing some sort of mental calculation, and she was: running back over a day of symptoms. As she continued, a fear surfaced behind her eyes, and then she was wracked by a pain that arched her back again. With it, her skin and lips went pale. When it was over, she said through a tremble, "Conover. It's not his time yet."

"You mean—? Should I fetch the midwife? Cecily?"

"Yes, Conover. Put on a kettle of water and fetch the midwife as quickly as you can. She may yet be able to soothe him." She said this as she heaved herself from the chair and made her way toward their bed. "I'll just lie down and rest."

He thought it was over. But when he returned with the midwife, both of them panting, the midwife said, "Maybe it is the child's time." And his wife said through gritted teeth, "Now I need you to go and protect it." She didn't say what, not in front of the midwife, but although he knew exactly *what* she was referring to, he was about as confused about what he should do as if he didn't know she meant the ring at all.

He stood on the stone outside their closed front door. It was a deeply dark night: the clouds veiled all the stars on a moonless night. A square of weak, bouncing glow fell from a window of the cottage onto the ground in the front yard. Back toward the town, there would be lights flickering here and there, squares of it and swinging points of it. Out toward the farms, there was a sudden spot of blaze marking a distant homestead. Conover's eyes were drawn straight ahead to the blackness that cloaked the fields, the rolling hills, and the distant Branderby Woods. Normally the delineations were lost on a dim night in a pressing darkness. But tonight, straight ahead, a winking point of orange shone where Conover knew the edge of the Woods met the hills only by the familiarity of its height and an almost imperceptible quality of reflection on overhanging trees. It was small seen from here, and yet the flames must be towering. In a darkness as full as tonight's, the light glared at him, catching in his eyes.

Then something else drew his attention, and he looked north to see another fire somewhere up along the curve of the distant Woods. It was even farther, but the night made it easy to see it, shining there in the oblivion. Conover thought to look south, swung his head, and was rewarded with the sight of another distant fire, another orange light at the edge of the Woods.

The farmers were calling them *fairy fires*. They had appeared straight out of legend, on this ghostly night, and Conover didn't know what to make of them. Their oddity was just something else to make him uneasy, something else for Dion to stick in his portents pipe and smoke it. In fact though, they were not fairy fires at all. They had been lit by the farmers themselves: Laurent, Kori,

Manno, and Otho. It was their idea to draw eyes outward from the cottages and hovels of the farmland, away from the castle toward the mysterious bonfires curled up in the embrace of the mysterious, foreboding forest.

¤

Aren was an excellent sneak. According to his disposition, he burgled without stooping or slinking. He was a tall, thin, aloof man, and he did not stoop. He walked quietly between light, floated upright from one noticeable moment to the next, often with a steady, smooth pace. This is how he approached the dark alley in the Outer Circle, how he walked down it with hardly a footfall, how he slipped undetected into the shadows at the alley's end.

The shadows at the end of the alley dissolved into what appeared to be an inconsequential crevice in a stone wall, an architectural anomaly between two buildings. Aren pushed his way through that crack, the rock scraping at his arms in the dark. He emerged in a small, claustrophobic, square opening that yawned high above to a sky that was invisible in its blackness. Out of the sky, a fresh breeze fell, rapidly cooling the space. Aren felt around, letting his eyes adjust, until he grasped a low, narrow grate on the opposite side from where he had entered. Then he groped again until he found a keyhole and thrust a key in.

The lock did not give easily. Aren had no idea how frequently— if ever—a secret castle entrance might be used. After all, the point was for it to be secret, used only for the queens and princesses and baby princes to escape invaders. The little, grated door also did not give easily, and it creaked obnoxiously in the night, scraping over the uneven stones. How could their plan survive two, three times opening this door tonight?

He yanked the door closed behind him, placed the key back in the lock, and locked the door. Then he stood in the pitch black, the dank air, and a small pool of standing water to wait.

A while later, Berenice huffed and puffed like a clumsy bear into the stone opening. He groped around at the walls until he found the grate, then stuck his face close to it, and gasped out in a whisper, "Aren?"

Aren could smell the terror on Berenice's breath. He could also hear it in his voice, in his breathing, in his slobbering. With his eyes adjusted as well as a man's will in such a dark space, Aren could also see the ghostly outlines of Berenice's eyes, wide and rolling.

"Yes, I am here," Aren said. "Now stand back and let me open the gate." Aren unlocked it, pushed it open with another deafening screech and scraping, and moved aside to let Berenice into the tunnel. They could not fit side-by-side, so they thinned themselves out as Berenice pushed by.

Berenice stood, now ahead, in the tunnel, looking all about himself at nothing. "Go on," Aren prompted. "Just follow that tunnel until it comes up on the other side of the Green Moat. Hilary will be there." Aren backed out of the door, shoved it closed, and locked Berenice in, disappearing with the key.

The rat could have left me the key, Berenice thought. "In fact, I think he was supposed to." He said this out loud, but the quality of his voice in the cramped, drippy place did not comfort him in any way. He adjusted his cloak over his shoulders, felt for his satchel, and put one foot in front of the other, groping ahead along the walls with his hands. *This has to be the worst work. I deserve more than a thirty-second, that's for sure.*

It was a long and uncomfortable walk into the earth at a gentle slope down and then back up again under the castle. When he emerged up a rough-hewn staircase, the open space was just as dark.

Berenice heard only a rustle before he was hit over the head with an extremely weighty candelabra.

He went down in a heap, and Hilary was glad that his body did not tumble down the stairs, but lay where she felled him.

In the small, dark room—more like a cave underneath the main apartments of the castle—Hilary lit a lantern and used its light to search Berenice's body for a vial. It was in his satchel, and she took the whole bag, looping its strap up over her head and an arm before leaving out a wooden door and continuing up through the castle's passageways. Berenice was still breathing.

She imagined that her next job would be much simpler in reality than in theory. The kingdom had deliberately trained her in the art of seduction and illusion, and that would be the easiest way to bring a glass of wine to the crypt guard and get him to drink it with promises she never intended to keep. She would watch his eyelids droop and his body get heavier and heavier until he slumped asleep at her feet. She would defeat her second man of the night, leaving him lying there unprotected from the consequences as she stepped agilely over him, knife in hand, to cut through The Queen's well-oiled shroud.

◻

Lykus thought that perhaps in his enthusiasm for Hilary he had volunteered for too much. He had already drugged the castle and sent everyone off to dreamland. Now here he was in the dead of night tripping down the path from the kitchens to the store sheds, as blind in the dark as a mole, stealing a bag of rice from the King. And that wasn't the half of it. Oh no, not the half of it. How had it fallen to him to do the very worst bit?

He unlatched the familiar door and let himself into the shed closest to the castle, closing it behind him. What use was leaving it open? There was no light to be found anywhere, even in the heavens. He groped at the shelf on his left, where he had stored the bag of rice. Then he hefted it off the shelf and let himself back out the way he came in.

He moved slowly around the outside of the castle, clinging to its base as much as possible. He crashed through manicured shrubs and navigated high weeds. It took longer than his trial run, that was for sure, but Lykus' slow pace would give Berenice time to poison the crypt guard. Lykus wondered what he would do if the guard was standing there, merrily guarding the crypt, wide awake. The idea made his stomach twist. He supposed he would have to crouch in the grass and the dark and wait for Berenice. But what if Berenice never came? What if the tincture simply had not worked?

Creeping and stumbling around in the chilly blackness of a deep night, Lykus' heart suddenly reached out for Hilary. He kept walking.

He slowed as he approached the final wall before the crypt entrance. He worked his way up to it. Then he peered around a corner, letting his eyes adjust to the light of a single torch mounted at the crypt's entrance. Sure enough, a burly guard had been reduced to a snoring pile of bones, muscles, and armor just outside the gate. Lykus moved into the light. He stepped around the guard and laid a hand on the gated door. He took his eyes off the guard and a thrill of surprise ran down his spine. The gate was ajar. He knew it was supposed to be unlocked, but surely the guard would not have been guarding an open gate all night? That meant it had been opened after the guard was poisoned.

Panic mounted in his stomach.

Lykus eased the bag of rice down to his feet and entered the crypt. He took the torch as he went, picking his way down the stairs and into a space he had never been before. Stephyn had mapped it all out for him: a roomy cave for the main room, surrounded by niches and tunnel entrances branching off in several directions. The implement tables, the hanging sconces, and a long, chest-high slab in the middle, where The Queen lay dead, resolute, perfumed, vulnerable. His fears propelled him forward quickly, and he stopped right beside her, his eyes drawn to the place—from Stephyn's map—where Lykus was to make the incision in the shroud to retrieve the ring.

With his knife still concealed in his tunic, Lykus held the torch aloft and gaped down with incredulity. The tautness of the oily fabric had pulled a careful slit wide, revealing only a dark, empty, gaping hole, as black as the night.

¤

Nikeas leaned his upper body out over the edge of the promenade. Except for a couple of towers, which he had already visited tonight, this was the highest point in the kingdom. What kingdom? It was engulfed in the thick, starless night. He could see lights here and there as far as the edge of the wood, and then nothing, not even ground or sky. It looked like Kentwend was completely alone with its secrets tonight.

A gust of wind hit Nikeas squarely, blowing his pale hair back from his white face, but his shoulders and his head remained unmovable. He looked down over the parapets, down, down to the grounds at the back side of the castle proper. He searched for movement in the vast chasm that represented the kitchens, the gardens, and there, way off to the right, the path to the crypt. He listened to Rufus and Linos behind him, whispering together with faltering voices, waiting for a guard to stir or a shout to rise up on the wind. What a couple of knuckleheads. Like they could quell an uprising without him or soothe a doubt into submission. He supposed they looked intimidating enough, even to most of the soldiers, flanking the prince as he appeared suddenly out of the dark on the promenade.

There! Nikeas' gaze caught on the slightest movement directly below him—so directly that it made Nikeas dizzy to scrutinize it. But scrutinize he did, squinting into the dark and listening to the breaking of twigs and the rustle of leaves as Lykus hunched along the base of the wall. Nikeas watched him for a long time. Lykus became lost in the dark and silence, and then Nikeas would find him again, further along. Once or twice Nikeas turned on his heels suddenly and walked off into the night, Rufus and Linos scrambling to follow. Then Nikeas stopped again at a different spot along the promenade and looked thoughtfully over the edge of the wall, tracking Lykus.

Nikeas watched from above, as Lykus entered the crypt. Lykus emerged too soon after, running from the crypt with his brown robes trailing out behind him. Lykus ran, and Nikeas once again turned to go, but this time, he moved so fast up the promenade that Rufus and Linos were left behind.

¤

First the fairy fires, then the street show, and now a crazy man being pulled on a cart through the Outer Circle? A moonless night, a starless night. Summer went round the bend with autumn on its heels. Cecily was right. This was a portentous night.

Conover watched the cart struggle down the road, as he walked backward along the path. Then he hurried off over the stone road bisecting the Green Moat. He was scarcely off the bridge and into the castle's courtyard when a guard at the gate called out to him, "Who goes there?"

Conover felt something hostile in the voice. Of course, when had Conover come unbidden to the castle under the cover of night? Perhaps the castle viewed this type of behavior as inherently suspicious. He continued to scuttle toward the guard and called back, "It is Conover the Storykeeper."

"State your business!"

Conover now approached the guard directly but kept a respectful distance maybe ten ells short. The guard was a noble-looking man, outfitted in his soldier's uniform, his face fallen into deep delineations of light and shadow, bouncing slightly with the flicker of the few torches. His hair was salt and pepper under his dayhelm. Conover thought he had met him before.

Then Conover realized, with a great fall of the heart, how complicated his simple plan had really been. "I—, I have a message for the King." He finished by standing taller and altering his voice to feign authority.

"No one in tonight. Royal order."

This sounded to Conover like more magic and mayhem, but it also sounded like he wouldn't be walking in through the Main Gate. He tried again, anyhow. "But I am the Storykeeper, and it is the proper time to tell the King—"

"*Not* the proper time." Herman's large, rolling voice rang out into the night.

"Yes, yes I see." Conover took one step backward and lowered his head, looking down at his hands as he thought.

"I'll be going, then. I'll come back tomorrow." Herman still stood erect and unwavering, but he sighed—*with relief?*—as Conover turned to retreat.

Conover exited the courtyard on its far right side and then turned right. He imagined that, to the guard this looked like Conover was keeping on the path, and hopefully Herman would stop watching when the Storykeeper left the low light. Instead, Conover curved off the path with the wall of the castle. He traced around the outside of it, moving with his back and the palms of his hands against it, picking his way along. What other sort of entrances would there be to the castle? Eventually the ground sloped downward, still keeping the vast green on the left, and a raised walkway loomed ahead, traversing the green.

Conover strained his eyes in the dark, studying where the pathway met the castle. Of course there was a guard there, up on the low bridge with more torches. Nothing else stirred. Conover crept forward, his pace slowed almost to a stop, watching the guard and scoping the ground before him. It dipped even further until it became uneven. Along the castle wall it rose to the top of the bridge, and slightly to the left, it nestled into an overshadowed corner at the intersection of raised walkway and berm. Conover left the wall and crawled toward this deeply dark corner.

As he approached, eyeing the top of the bridge the whole time, he heard a "Psst!"

Conover's heart quickened until he told himself, *It's just a drunk in the shadow of the bridge.* He crept forward, now staring into the darkness, trying to identify anything. "Psst!" It came again in the smallest of whispers on the breeze. "Is that you, Conover?" Now Conover stopped. "Yes," he squeaked, uncertainty coating the one word.

"It's me. Dion. Come quickly, under here!" Dion's voice was just a hiss, but Conover was still sure it was Dion's. Conover scrambled the remaining few ells toward the shadowed corner, watching up at the guard's post. Then he slumped into the stone wall with his shoulder and caught his breath, trying to calm his racing heart. He could feel Dion's presence beside him, his breath even in the silence.

"Dion, you scared me! I thought you were going to murder me. Or turn me in." Conover turned to Dion, and their conversation was barely audible, even to themselves. It was more moving lips than breath.

"Did you get my message?"

"Why do you think I'm crawling around out here. You mean... They wouldn't even let the Oracle in?"

"No, but I wasn't surprised."

"But do you think that means the soldiers are in on

something?"

"Well, some of them. Or maybe just those who give the orders. Or maybe the castle is as suspicious as we are. Seems bold, if there is going to be a murder or uprising or whatever. What do you think this is, anyhow?"

"A robbery." If Cecily was right about the night, perhaps she was right that the ring was in danger as well.

"What would make a robbery so important? Why would there be signs?"

"Magic," was all Conover said before a shout from overhead stopped them cold. It was a soldier by the sound of him; whether the guard or not, they weren't sure. They crouched and listened for something, for an opportunity to get in the castle, which would come later when they surfaced at the path's base and were conscripted to heft buckets. But for now, they just sat and listened to the shouts increase, to the castle door opening and closing over and over again, and to a cart roll over the path, sloshing with water in its great barrel. The scent of fire grew until the smokiness bit at their nostrils.

¤

The Sage had been walking in the night garden, headed toward the crypt, when something toward the kitchens caught his senses. He trod that direction instead and ended up in one of the sheds, which was currently on fire. He was drawn toward a back corner, where he found himself looking down at an empty space concealed under a bottom shelf. In it, he could sense papers and a couple vials, two of them tipped over on their sides, one completely spilled and the other slowly seeping onto the paper and the wood. The reaction between the two liquids had caused great heat to build, and what was once smoldering was now leaping flames.

He turned and walked back toward the crypt with more urgency but stopped short on the path from the sheds to the kitchen when he heard men behind him. He was not afraid of being detected, but he was suspicious of their behavior. They were whispering and hissing in alarmed tones, back and forth, and scuttling along the edges of the buildings. The Sage stood and listened as they approached.

"What do we do now?"

"I don't know! Go see the King?"

"Go see the King? You mean just pop on up to his room and waltz in and…"

"Well, perhaps if we wander, we'll come across someone…"

"Someone who might what? Get us an interview?"

"*Understand.*"

Then, standing directly before them on their progress toward the castle's gardens, The Sage straightened up and said very forcefully, "What is your business here?"

"Aaarrgggaacckk!" is what Conover said, and looked away as he threw his arms to shield his face. Dion stood amazed, and gently whispered, "The Sage!"

There they stood—one trembling and cowering, one gaping—as The Sage asked, "Do we know each other?" He looked curiously at Dion.

"I'm the Oracle," Dion smiled.

"Ah. That explains it." The Sage smiled back, as if to an old friend.

Conover spoke from his stricken position, "We have come to help!" There was no use in whispering anymore.

"You are firemen?"

"He is the Storykeeper." Dion nodded his head to Conover, who was only relaxing inch by inch.

"You usually come to fight fires?"

Dion said, "I had insight. I knew there was something stirring in the deep in Kentwend. And I told my friend of it. I believe his wife sent him." His eyes twinkled with mirth, and Conover sulked at Dion.

"And the insight led you here?"

"Conover," Dion indicated the Storykeeper, "his wife went into labor, and early. It was a sign. She sent him out to speak to the King. We were turned back from the castle, and both of us were sure that meant we were right. Then we were asked to help with the fire—" He rushed forward with his explanation. "We wanted to make sure The King and The Queen were all right."

The Sage's wooden face twitched for a brief moment at the mention of The Queen. "But The Queen is dead," he answered.

"We respect her body. We respect the ring."

"Ah, the ring." A connection was made in The Sage's mind. He took a step toward the men and softened his posture while sinking into deep thought. Distractedly, he said, "You may think it is men afoot tonight, but I can almost guarantee it *is the ring*." He smiled at the men as he extended a hand to them. "And I think it's best if we all let it run its course. Do one of you have a bowl of soup and a pillow for a weary traveler?"

"But the ring—"

"I understand now. Despite my transcendence, I am yet human enough in these wants: to not waste life and to prevent it from spilling. This night, on the other hand, is a matter of magic and objects. These I tend to merely observe and note, not to interfere."

Conover looked up at The Sage with a look of consternation. "That's what I told my wife!"

"Really?" The Sage raised his eyebrows at Conover.

"Well, almost," he mumbled. "I told her it wasn't the Storykeeper's place to interfere."

"I'm sure she had her own argument."

"Oh, she did." They stood for a moment, the flames behind

them licking higher while a suffocating smoke grew thicker. Conover asked, "Did you just magically appear here?"

The Sage said, "I have been in the Woods, watching."

"And you haven't come near?"

"Well, you're one for questions."

"I'm the Storykeeper."

"Right. I'll watch what I say in front of you, then. I did come into Kentwend and onto the castle grounds, but I was not recognized. One of the princesses reported me as a peasant ruffian. She sicced a hound on me." He looked injured.

Conover apparaised The Sage's clothes. "Yes, well you didn't do much to convince her, did you?"

"No. I did not."

Dion, who had glanced a few times over his shoulder, broke in. "Excuse me, fellows. But we have a robbery in progress and half the castle on fire. Mightn't we, you know, help? Gather stories later?"

Conover coughed. "Oh, yes, of course. Right."

"Well?" asked The Sage.

"Well?" Conover ogled him. "What should we do? It's you two who know everything!"

"Hmm." The Sage closed his eyes, screwed up his face, and raised his hands. He started mumbling in an unrecognized language.

Conover whispered, "Are you seeing the future?"

The Sage dropped his hands and snapped open his eyes. "Of course not. I was just having one over on you. Now, I believe that I will head up to the castle's sleeping quarters and make sure everyone is out all right. After that, I would appreciate that meal and pillow from one of you."

⌧

Panther made his debut in the first act of the street show, then disappeared into the night along with the coins of several of the audience members. As he went, he met Brom's wink and he nodded, then looked over at Bricteva and the long line of her neck as she turned wildly in a circle. He thumbed the key in his deep pocket, turning it over and over.

He walked quickly along the streets of the town and through the Outer Circle, coming up on the south side of the castle, where he stalked brazenly up the bridge, a lone man in the night. Musa must have been successful; the torch was extinguished and Bernhard, the guard, was likely down with her in the shadow of the walls in the thick bushes that lined this section of the Green Moat. Panther approached the door under cover of darkness, inserted the key in the hole, unbolted the lock, removed the key, and turned and walked away. He didn't cross the bridge on his way back but turned to the left and dissolved into shadow on the Green Moat. He lay down in the grass, folding his long arms behind his head for a pillow. He was far away enough from the road and bridge that no one would see him in the oppressive dark. He was close enough to the bushes that he could listen to Musa and the guard and also keep an eye on the door.

Over the castle wall, in the garden, Nikeas had come crashing out of a back door of the castle's main building into a thicket of trees and shrubbery, heading off Lykus. "Lykus!" he called in his most forceful, authoritative whisper. Lykus looked wild-eyed over his shoulder and quickened his stumbling pace. "Lykus! It's Prince Nikeas! Stop!" It was not working, and Nikeas had to run after Lykus and tackle him to the cold ground in the center of The Queen's walking garden. Nikeas sat on Lykus and held the Cupbearer's wrists as he struggled, grunting and panting.

"Lykus! What's happening?" Nikeas hissed out of his teeth, his face so close Lykus could smell his perfume, the soap on his skin, and the oil in his hair.

Lykus's struggle slackened slowly. Finally, he stopped. Sagging, he answered, "The ring wasn't there."

"What do you mean, the ring wasn't there?!"

"I went in to get it." He whimpered between each painful statement. "The gate was open. The shroud was already cut. There was nothing in the hole. Nothing on her hand."

Nikeas stared for a moment blankly over Lykus' shoulder at the ground. Then he shook the man by his shoulders. "You have it, don't you? You have the ring, you dirty,"—hitting his head against the ground—"lying,"—hitting it again—"bastard!" and again.

Lykus curled his body up as tightly as he could with Nikeas on top of him and started weeping great big sobs. "Please!" he begged, forgetting to whisper. "Please!"

"Shut up!" Nikeas hissed. He roughly patted Lykus down, searching his pockets. Nikeas straightened up and stared off into the darkness. Lykus still moaned and whimpered, rolling his head side to side. After a minute, Nikeas stood, dusted off his front, and spat out a disgusted, "Stand up, you old fool." Lykus remained sniveling on the ground, relieved of the news he had been carrying.

Nikeas turned and headed out a door in the castle wall—where Musa and Panther both heard him and Panther dropped in to trail behind, unseen—down the south bridge, and into a nearby alley in the Outer Circle.

Nikeas was physically stopped as he came round the corner by a small, muscular, sinewy man with a stink of musk and sweat on him. At first all Nikeas could see were flashes of black, curly hair, a felt hat, and glinting jewelry, but then he backed away and yelled, "Take your hands off me!"

Tarquis stepped back with a shove and mumbled at Nikeas to shut up or he was going to get them all caught, prince or no prince. The two squared off and glared through the dark. "What are *you* doing here, anyway? Shouldn't you be dreaming sweetly in your perfumed bed?"

Nikeas held his gaze, looking down over the bridge of his nose. He answered, "The ring is gone. Go on home, if you have one." He heard a feminine gasp from inside the alley. He looked over Tarquis's shoulder and saw the wagon with its horses facing away from them. The horses snorted and pawed at the ground, and the shadowy outline of a woman stood in the seat of the wagon.

Tarquis looked back into the alley, then back at Nikeas. Doubt overwhelmed his features as he asked, "What d'you mean? Where is it?"

"I don't know. Tell Theobald that someone intercepted us." Then, after a blank look, "Someone. Took. It. Before. Lykus. Got. There."

"I know what intercepted means."

There was a series of knocks and jostling at the cart before Irene appeared, just her face, over Tarquis' shoulder. She was dressed for traveling. "But—," she said as she put a gloved hand on Tarquis's shoulder. He shrugged it off. There was more bumping and swishing at the cart, and Nikeas raised his eyebrows at Tarquis. Maram appeared on the bed of the cart, standing over the three of them with hay stuck in her hair and clothing. She trailed a wool blanket behind her.

"Maram, get back in there." Tarquis turned, just as Nikeas asked, "What is she doing here?"

"Nothing," Tarquis spat. "Just a stowaway."

Maram did not appreciate the flat tone in Tarquis' voice. She squared her shoulders and stated, "We're leaving, Tarquis and I. Together."

"Well," Irene stepped in, "all of us."

"No." This was said by an unembodied voice at the other side of the alley. They all turned to look but could see nothing, and waited as footsteps approached. "*Not* all of you. J-just them. Irene, you m-m-ight as well hand over the travel money now. You are about to b-be robbed anyhow and d-dumped in Niska, while your best friend and this *pirate* run off together. Of course, you know, *she* c-c-c-an't last long, either. *Anyhow*," Kyros had now moved close enough that if they didn't know his stuttering whine already, they could tell who he was by sight.

"You," looking at Irene, "will be able to go b-back and p-ply the same story you cooked up for Maram; that the t-t-two of you were abducted and only one of you escaped." Irene's eyes were now wide with terror and growing wider as she looked from Kyros to Tarquis to Maram. "*Except...*" he feigned confusion and thought, "that won't work... because I'm going to expose b-both of you as liars and thieves and b-*both* of your families will be leaving town, d-disgraced and blackmailed, *together*. Like old t-t-times? Together forever? In p-p-prison?"

Tarquis gave Kyros a sideways look. "What does any of this have to do with you, old man?"

"The ring and the g-g-girl are a t-trade for a house in the Outer Circle: M-m-maram's house."

"Who? Who would trade for Maram?"

"The Qu-Queen of the Underground, who d-d-did you think?"

"Why does she want Maram?"

"Why should I care? I d-don't."

"Is it she who has the ring? Farrah took it?"

A look of doubt flickered over Kyros's face. "The ring—?"

"The ring. Farrah stole it?"

"No. *I'm* stealing the ring." Kyros faltered in his demeanor now, as well. "The ring is *here*."

Nikeas looked at the failing courtier, twisted the knife into his point of pain by mocking him. "N-n-no. It's n-n-not."

"But all this—!" Kyros regained himself but not completely. "I'm sure you're a cheat and a liar," looking pointedly at Tarquis and not at the Prince. "Get in your c-carriage and g-go! B-but you are leaving Maram *and* the ring here."

Tarquis laughed, but then Maram called out, "Merek!" He looked up at her, and she said, "Let's just go now. Irene can stay here, where she's safe."

Kyros said, "No, she stays here," and at the same time, Irene said, "Maram? How could you?"

When Tarquis reamined silent, Maram turned to Irene. "We were going to keep you safe, Irene. Send you back with the wagon."

Kyros snickered. "But not the ring, see? They would have pushed your body from the back of their love nest."

Maram made a grab for Irene, but everyone froze when they heard approaching noises out in the street. Wooden wheels ground the stone, and men's voices shouted. Tarquis looked to Kyros, and Maram and Irene both looked to Tarquis.

"That would b-be the soldiers I ordered," Kyros smiled. "They have no reason to d-detain a man with a c-c-cart. B-but they are very interested in the g-g-girls. So again, the ring for your freedom?"

"There's no ring, man!" Nikeas shouted.

"Give it to me!"

"I don't have it!"

"We don't have it!"

Tarquis turned perturbed to Irene, and she resisted only a little as he reached into her cloak and grabbed at a sachet of money. He tossed it to Kyros, who listened to it jingle before catching it and shoving it down into his pocket. Tarquis extended a hand toward Maram, who looked deep and questioning into his eyes and then over at Kyros and Nikeas before she was helped down to the ground. Maram made a grab for Tarquis as he turned, but he pushed her off, saying, "Just go home. The jig is up."

"You can't leave me with this man! He'll ruin me!"

"I would have ruined you, too."

Tarquis quickly mounted the wagon, gathered the reigns, and pulled away. The cart swayed and creaked as the two ladies stood watching, hugging themselves, as it disappeared into the dark.

¤

At the edge of the Branderby Woods, where a road wound from the back of the castle out through the town and farms and hills and disappeared into the thick trunks and branches, a fairy fire burned off the road. Kori tended it, working to draw nocturnal wanderers over to his bonfire, over to a hot drink or a story and an hour gazing into the flames. Earlier, there had been some travelers moseying out of town and into the woods: a caravan and a couple of men on foot. Were there always stragglers like this walking into the forest at night? Where did they go?

Night had somewhere become morning, but it was still dark, still oppressively dark, and Kori guessed the sun was still an hour or two off. He was aware he had nodded off, but he couldn't say exactly for how long. He shook his head to clear it, then forced himself up to stoke the fire, to throw more branches on the blaze. Just then, he heard another wagon coming up from town in the dark. A couple of horses clop-clopping, a few wheels churning at the dirt and the occasional stone, catching on the potholes. There, a single lantern light swayed from the front post. Kori should have seen it making its way here a half-hour ago. How long had he been asleep?

The carriage moved pretty fast. Perhaps Kori would have only seen it for mere minutes. Maybe the driver had only now put on the light. But how else could he drive on a starless night? While Kori wondered, the carriage came up fast, and he saw only a bent, unkempt man, thin and muscular, on the box, his hair flying out wild in the breeze he created in his haste. Then it all disappeared into the trees.

In a clearing only a short walk into the woods up the same road, a few men crouched in the grasses, adjusting their eyes over and over to nothing. They did not whisper. When they had whispered, earlier in the night, Farrah had snapped at them, and her coldness shut them up. It made them uneasy to have her here at all. She was not accustomed to sitting up nights in the woods, but that feeling in the air—the same one that was needling at her goons—had made her anxious as well. Anxious to pull off the job, to control it into success. And yet she scoffed at her own feelings, at the ridiculousness of being compelled to respond to something she couldn't calculate, something she hadn't reasoned out—magic. So there in the deep grass under the swaying branches of an interminable woods sat Farrah in a chair Aren had been forced to carry, her booted feet up on a stool that another man had been forced to carry, her thin-gloved hands folded on her lap, her steely eyes staring ahead, unseeing and unseen.

All of their ears pricked at the sound of an approaching wagon. This time of night, on this particular night, it must be Tarquis and Irene, making their way from Kentwend toward the closest village of mention, Niska. The men rose to their haunches, searching through the trees for the sign of a light. One of the men whistled, signaling another group of men behind a curtain of trees to mount their horses. As they did, the cart burst out of the wood into the clearing.

The men on foot ran back and forth in front of the wagon, scaring and confusing the horses and eventually stopping them. At the same time, the men on horseback rode up beside and behind, blocking the cart in. They all brandished weapons, which glinted in the lone flame from the lantern, making long, metallic *ping*s as they were unsheathed over the sound of the horses and the wheels and Tarquis yelling, "Woah, woah, woah!" and grunting back on the reigns. Tarquis was no stranger to heists, but he cursed the dark for allowing so few clues. Was this an average band of thieves, or were these men here because a little birdie told them to come?

He didn't have long to wait, tracking their movements and straining at the reigns, for his answer. Out of the dark obscurity of the clearing, a tall, frail figure emerged, revealing its femininity with each step she took into the flickering, swaying ring of light. *Farrah. He should have guessed long ago.*

"Well, Farrah the Barren, imagine meeting you here tonight." He had to shout over the spooked horses.

"Hand it over, Tarquis."

Tarquis grinned as he pronounced clearly, "There is nothing to hand over."

Farrah's face hardened. "Hand it over, *or else.*" Tarquis could sense the men all around him flexing their posture, leaning forward into their anticipation with a murmur.

Tarquis leaned back on the seat and crossed his feet as he lifted them up onto the running board. "As much as it would please me to oblige you, oh Barren One, there is nothing to give you. The ring has already been stolen."

Farrah blinked at Tarquis. "We'll have to make sure." She flicked her hand and immediately the men moved forward, surrounding the horses, the wagon, and Tarquis. Tarquis didn't bother to put up a fight but let himself be dragged down to the ground and searched roughly.

The ruckus of the search and beating alerted Kori, out at the fairy fire, that something was happening. He jumped up and ran off into the woods. Behind him, the fire, freshly stoked, blazed. A spark shot out with a dramatic *pop!* and landed in the tall grasses of the eastern Kentwend fields. A very mellow breeze made it glow, and a flame was born. The flame flickered, licked at the sky, and was encouraged as it consumed the blade of grass on which it had been born and then leapt to another blade nearby. It doubled and then multiplied until it had made a merry second bonfire there in the field. Then, with a shift of the wind, it spread out in a line that began to smoke heavily in the brightening dark.

Farrah sniffed at the air and put out her hands to stop the men who were now kicking Tarquis down on the ground, but it didn't work. They could barely see her in the dark, and their frenzy was too complete. They stayed this way for a while, the men kicking Tarquis and Farrah posed with her hands outstretched, palms down, and her nose to the air. Then a farmer came running out of the dark, yelling for them to stop, and Farrah saw it: there, through the trees, the mounting gleams of firelight as it spread wide against the forest.

◘

Lulu felt restless. She hadn't been outdoors all day, being diverted from writing to etiquette to reading to weaving, Ingrid eyeing her like a hawk. So Lulu was restless and cross and bored.

She had hardly eaten anything at all at dinner, slipping away from the table to escape Ingrid. But Ingrid had abandoned her own supper and shadowed her. Defeated, Lulu returned to her rooms, ordered a dinner she barely touched, and set to reading a particularly interesting and romantic book she had borrowed from the castle's library. Yet under the scrutinizing eyes of Ingrid and then Agnes it could not tantalize her, and she readied for bed early to escape her day.

She must have fallen asleep, for she remembered nothing of getting into bed. But she woke in the dark to hear Agnes leave the room and never return. Lulu lay there for hours, finding shapes in the darkness and studying the flashing patterns behind her eyelids. When she could not stay still a moment longer, she sat up in bed, groped about for her slippers and robe, and slid into them. It occurred to her that Agnes, who normally slept in a second niche in Lulu's room, must be *somewhere*. Suspicious, Lulu cracked open the door to the hallway very slowly and very quietly. She looked through the crack into the hall, where a couple of torches kept the way dimly lit. *Who keeps these torches going all night?* she wondered. *Do they ever go out?* She pushed the door a little wider, just wide enough to slide out, and moved one leg and one arm and a head through.

Agnes popped out of the dark, her voice dry and husky. "Princess! What are you doing here? At this hour?"

Lulu stepped out into the hall and shut the door carefully behind her. Then she heightened herself and looked nonchalant. "I guess I could ask the same thing of you."

"I—," Agnes' face flushed, visible even in the dark. "I am keeping an eye out, Lulu."

"Is that part of your job, Agnes?"

"Not usually, Lulu." It was no help heaping lie on lie. "I just couldn't sleep, so I thought I would stay out here. Just in case."

Lulu gave Agnes a long look with her head cocked, then seemed to decide that this conversation wasn't as interesting as other things. "Well, I'm going a-walk." She turned on her heels and sauntered off into the dark, toward a bend in the hall that featured a tall window.

"Lulu—!" Agnes croaked, but Lulu had already stopped at the casement and stood looking down. She whirled back around, facing Agnes, but Agnes had already noticed the play of firelight on Lulu's face and the thick swath of smoke that was coming in at the top of the window and sinking to the floor.

"Agnes!" yelled Lulu. "The kitchen sheds are on fire!"

"Princess!" yelled Agnes. There was a panic in Agnes' posture and an uncertainty. She hesitated before yelling, "Come with me! We must get out of here!"

"But Agnes; the others! We must wake the others!"

Agnes stood exactly where she was, wringing her hands and wailing that Lulu must come with her, while Lulu ran for the closest door. Just then, Nikeas dashed around the corner at the opposite end of the hall. He stopped, as did Lulu, when his eyes lighted on her, and then his gaze was drawn out the window closest to him.

"What is it?" Lulu asked, before yelling, "The kitchen sheds are on fire!"

"No." Nikeas looked at her with concern. "The eastern fields are on fire! Look."

Lulu ran quickly to him. "But Nikeas. The sheds, too. Go see." She pointed a long, white arm down the length of the hallway toward the opposite window. He ran up to it and looked down, just as she was looking out at the distant blaze.

"I must get you out of here to a safe house in the Outer Circle, until we can figure out what is happening." There was real fear in his look. "Wake the others!"

Agnes stopped wailing at this and looked imploringly at Nikeas. "But sir, they are all…"

His eyes caught hers, and they registered terror. "But—," he sputtered. Then he turned inward, thinking, and didn't notice that Lulu had already run off to wake the unwakeable.

¤

Cecily's labor was not long. In a few hours the baby had come, howling into the world to be wrapped in cloths and set next to his mother to nurse. Then mother and child fell into a deep, peaceful sleep. But after a short time, Cecily began to stir, and her mind roved over many things in her half-lucidity. Her dream must have been about the Baker's children, when they were still children. In many dreams she would save them from a flood or a storm or a sickness. She did not remember from which disaster she shielded them this time, but the dream bled into raving thoughts of tunnels underground and the same bed the boys had slept in, there among smooth walls of dirt. The tunnel was lit with a hundred sconces, and Cecily sat on the side of the bed, looking down into the wounded faces as she had first known them.

Rufus was ten. She told him the stories. She told him of the magic. It was the only time they listened to her like this, without a bitterness. She would tell her baby the same stories. Her baby...

She woke with a heave of panic in her chest, but quickly discovered that he was still there next to her. The midwife was seated nearby, watching and waiting. They smiled at each other in the light of the crackling hearth.

Cecily righted herself, leaning on the crook of her arm against the logs and a pillow. She watched over the baby. She dared not touch him and wake him, but his smooth cheeks called out for her kisses and caresses. He was well swaddled.

It was still dark when Kentwend came alive with shouts and cracks, with people rushing mad and horses whinnying and steaming from flared nostrils. The midwife warned Cecily not to rise, but she went to the door anyway. The world smelled charred, and an orange glow flickered behind the castle and off to its left. One wagon went by, then another, sloshing with barrels of water.

"Neighbor! Ho!" Cecily had wrapped herself in her shawl and cloak, and she limped down to the gate. "What has happened?"

The man yelled as he passed, "Dunno! But there's quite a fire up the eastern farms and the castle!"

The midwife was on Cecily's heels. She coaxed her back to the house, but Cecily only gathered up her shoes before limping back to the gate. "Watch him," she said. "I've got to find Conover. I sent him to its heart—"

With the midwife sputtering and grasping, Cecily hailed the next passing wagon and asked if she could climb aboard. "She's only just had a baby!" the midwife implored the farmer and his wife. They paid no attention to her while Cecily rolled onto the back ledge of the cart, groaning as she did. They navigated the cart in the dark, aimed at the inferno against an empty sky.

The wagons of rain water came one after another to the fields. They had the flames circled to the forest, and many of the old trees had caught the fire in their tangled branches.

The river was providing relief for the castle fire but not fast enough. The heat and smoke licked into all the windows, and wooden beams, furniture, and linens spread the blaze from room to room above the kitchens and into the living chambers.

Nikeas had ushered Lulu and Agnes out onto the Main Bridge before rushing back inside. He wondered what he was going to do there. The impulse to save his mother's body was sickened by his desire of the ring. Still, he found himself outside of the crypt, standing and staring at the open gate, the felled guard, and the discarded bag of rice. Behind him someone moved, and he whirled around to come face to face with the Traveler, Blaise.

"You!" Nikeas spit it at him.

"You!"

After a moment, Blaise said, "I didn't start this fire!"

"And I didn't come to steal the ring!" It was a half-truth, anyway. "But you did!"

Nikeas launched himself at Blaise, and they went down together, hard. They rolled in a heap at the head of the stairs, arms and fists thumping into muscle and bone, hair yanked by the handful. In the desperate fight, they teetered on the top stair and then crashed down the staircase, head over feet over head over feet. At the bottom, they continued to swing and bite at each other, kicking and cussing on the stone floor at the foot of The Queen's death dais.

Blaise struggled to stand, but Nikeas grabbed at him and yanked him from the waist. In the movement, Blaise pulled at the mummy and it inched over the edge of the stone slab. Nikeas jumped up, ready to right it, and Blaise escaped him. Blaise had seen by the light of the still-burning torch Lykus had left behind that the ring had already been stolen. So Blaise ran back up the steps.

He did not stop in the garden but ran out the garden gate and over the southern bridge. On the road that fringed the Green Moat, he fell into a trot, and then into a loping gait. He shoved his hands into his pockets to finger the random prizes he had taken in his nocturnal roam of the castle. Still, his heart sank when he thought of the ring. He spat on the road. He limped forward in the hellish night, in the flickering of growing fires, in the smell of sulfur and burn, bruised and battered and angry.

Ahead, the Main Bridge arched toward the castle. As Blaise approached, the crowd gathering there expanded. Below, on the Moat, peasants and courtiers clustered for gossip. On the Bridge overhead, guards stood sentinel at the end, keeping the peasants and courtiers far from those who lived in the castle and had spilled out onto the Bridge.

The castle inhabitants quickly realized that their tight knot included a dozen or so people who did not even remotely belong in the castle. The truth was these people had been there for some time before the fire, some of them for hours. They were in the thieving loop, and they had come to be closer to the action. Now they were trapped. No one looked very comfortable with the accommodations.

But they were not long distracted by each other, as most of them quickly missed someone or something that was left inside and might soon be reduced to cinders. The stream of people from the castle was just beginning to dwindle. Agnes slumped out of the Main Gate with Teva leaning heavily across her shoulders. Both of them were dirty and tattered, and Agnes tottered under the weight. A soldier rushed forward to take the injured princess. King Jaden crashed out of the kitchen-side door to the Great Hall and strode through the room with a half-dozen kitchen servants in his wake. He coughed as he appeared before them, the lines on his face deepened with soot and sweat beading on his forehead below his skewed crown.

The King looked around at the crowd, at Teva slumped into the soldier, at the Baker looking shamefaced so close to the edge of the bridge he might jump, at the lanky pickpocket holding the hand of that half-dressed street performer, at the bull-sized Traveler nursing a burnt hand and the other tawny, unkempt Traveler cooing to him.

The King bellowed, "What on earth is going on here?"

A silence fell over the crowd, and they all looked to him. But no one offered an explanation. The flames licking the sky behind the King were an explanation of sorts, but that wasn't the half of it. In the tense hush, a cart approached the mouth of the Bridge with a clatter of wheels and the whinnying of a horse. A murmur rose from the crowd beyond the guards, and a farmer and a guard shouted to each other incomprehensibly. A woman was lifted from the cart and shoved into the arms of the guard, who turned to look at the royals, at a loss for what to do.

The King bellowed again. "Now what is it?"

The guard shouted up the bridge. "This farmer says this woman is sick, and he has no claim to her. She says her husband is in the castle."

"What?!"

The guard shrugged, still holding the woman, who was limp and whose dress, shawl, and cloak hung to the ground.

The King heaved an enormous sigh. "Well! Lulu, go and find out where that woman belongs! Any able men here must continue to clear the castle! You!" He was addressing Ingrid. "Find out who is unaccounted for!"

As the King turned his back to look to the castle, Conover rushed out with a page at his heels and a kitchen girl in his arms. He was handing her off to a chambermaid when he noticed something peculiar about the guard at the end of the bridge. The guard held a bundled person laying in his arms and there was something wrong with it. With the kitchen girl no longer in Conover's arms, he walked forward through the crowd, his eyes on the bundle.

It was Cecily! It had to be! Yet it couldn't be! He ran up the Bridge and threw himself at the guard, snatching the woman from him. It *was* Cecily. She was weak but she was awake, and she looked to him with immense relief and a painful pleading. His eyes roved over her, looking for what was wrong.

"But Cecily——! The baby?" He had noticed that while her stomach was still bulging, it was flabby and greatly recessed. Conover looked at Cecily, excruciating pain dawning on him.

"No!" she said. "No! He's fine, Conover. It's a boy."

"But where is he?"

"With the midwife."

"So why are you here?" Then he knew, without her saying. He wanted to shake her for leaving their baby and putting herself in such danger, but he also wanted to kiss her. So he kissed her: a suffocating, intense kiss that lasted and lasted and baffled the onlookers.

But their intruding gazes were kept only for a minute, because another man tripped out of the castle, looking badly beaten and afraid. Several of the people who did not, for one second, belong on the Bridge surged forward and surrounded him. Berenice looked around dazed at Rufus, Bricteva and Panther, Brom and Butrus, Seti and Raban and Drakon, and at Hero, and he seemed to grow smaller. With their bodies circling around him, he whispered, "I don't know where it is. Someone came out of the dark and knocked me out. They stole the poison. I never got to the crypt."

They wanted to know more, so they settled to speculating in pairs, whispering until they felt they were acting suspiciously.

Dion, who had just emerged from the castle, eyed the rough dozen, then with a word the King sent him back inside. They had already emptied the south wing, and as Dion dashed through the Great Hall, The Sage passed him by with an unconscious concubine over each shoulder. He grunted under the strain but waved Dion on.

Dion found a wider, circling staircase that led to a spacious and lavishly decorated hall. He ducked under the ceiling of smoke. With a groom on his tail, Dion pointed, and the groom nodded that he had seen the door at the far end, already ablaze. They rushed toward the closest door, but it opened on its own, crashing back on its hinges.

A man burst out, tugging at the hand of a young woman. His face was covered with his arm, and smoke billowed from the room behind him. As the man lowered his arm, Dion saw the Heir, Brando, through the soot and terror. Brando shoved the woman up the hall toward Dion, yelling, "Go!" She fled with the groom leading her, and Brando ran up the hall to the next door. It was open, and he was crashing out of it by the time Dion gained on him.

"She's gone!" Brando yelled. Then he turned and rushed to the next door. He had to shove himself against it to get it to open. The heat that billowed out blasted him back and his body hit the ground hard. Brando had the sense that a man was helping him up. He rushed back at the door, but the surging flames repelled him. He was about to rush into them when the man came at him again, grabbed him, and dragged him away.

The room belonged to the young princes. Fedel was gone, but his sons were trapped! The room was completely engulfed in flames. There could have been nothing alive in it. The fire consumed everything, reduced it to a radiance that in the morning would be a paltry pile of ash. And yet, unseen, across the room, on the narrow balcony, a mother held a child to her. Her arms encircled the child so that he was buried, only his eyes visible, squinting above a bare arm. She leaned forward, her bottom on the railing and her toes hanging over the tops of the garden trees.

Below her, Felix waved to her and screamed for her to jump. Behind her, the heat licked at her, the flames singeing her hair and dissolving the hems of her night dress. She could never make the jump. Neither could Osmund; he was too little. Felix had only made it by a miracle; he had practically flown to the soft bush that caught him. She looked down at him, his face smudged and golden in the firelight. He waved to her. "Mother! Jump!"

Fedel's face was an abstract mess of tears and soot. Her hair cascaded like a curtain to the side of her face, down over Osmund's head, shielding her terrified eyes from the world. She swung her back out over the emptiness and fell, like falling into bed, cradling Osmund above her.

Afterword

Hilary waited for the panic, riots, and emotion to dissipate, and for the harvest season to settle into its usual rhythm. The winter was drawing close, so Dion said, but there was yet no smell or feel of it in the air. Hilary chose the day of the baby Cecil's ceremony to slip out of the castle, over the Green Moat, over the water moat and the Dacidava, and toward Niska. She went on foot, huddled up in the peasant clothes she had collected, with a fabric bag slung over her shoulder full of bedding and food and a few things that she could sell. The rest of her valuables were sewn into her dress, her underskirts, even hidden in the heels of her shoes. The ring was sewn into the padding of her dress at her navel. She carried a knife at her hip, which made a noise against a cup as she walked.

As she neared the Branderby Woods over the still-blackened and desolate ground, she heard carriages approaching behind her.

She moved off the road to let them pass, buried her dirtied face and ratted hair in her arm. The carriages swayed as they went slowly by, heavy with all the Third Courtier's earthly possessions, his family, and his few remaining servants. Hilary marveled at all the parchments that were rolled and stacked into the back carriage, and the Courtier's women, huddled together and staring blankly out the back toward Kentwend, tears carving sparkling lines down their painted cheeks.

After they went, Hilary turned one last time to see the castle, the town, the farmland, everything in the palm of the forest's hand. She shuddered, for now she could see toward the north of the farmlands, where a scene was crystallized on a hill close to the town. There, five gallows stood tall and sticklike against the softness of brown, rolling meadow. The bodies—at this distance, just flotsam swaying in the wind—still hung as a reminder that would stick all winter long. With Nikeas as the little bird in Jaden's ear, they had executed the Travelers very quickly, and they had not spared even the woman.

THE END

PREVIEW OF

THE JOURNEY OF CLEMENT FANCYWATER

EXCERPT FROM CHAPTER TWO:

AN ARCHAEOLOGIST, A MARINE BIOLOGIST, AND AN ASTRONAUT

Clement didn't know that he slept.

He was awakened by the glow of the slow breaking of an ominously swirling-clouded dawn. He was surprised to find himself still face-up on the bench in exactly the position in which he must have fallen asleep. He was damp, uncomfortable, cold. His joints and back were sore. Then again, he felt rested, finally. He was hungry and thirsty.

With a jolt he realized that Judith would be looking for him this morning. He had played right into her hands! He sat up so fast a rush of blood made the world spin. And there, in the spinning world, came a man shuffling across the alcove. The man grunted an "All right, there, soldier," as Clement strained to focus on him. He wore cargo pants that were mud-caked at the bottom, grease-stained at the top, and about as old as dirt and a tattered, navy-blue hoodie over a threadbare, plaid button-up shirt. The hoodie was pulled up over his black, unruly, shoulder-length hair. A full beard and moustache hid a dirty, olive face with bulbous features and a large mouth. He carried a plastic grocery bag that hung limp with only a few, heavy items.

Clement hastened to gather up his own bag, his own sweatshirt, and his vest-pillow, and to shove everything else back down in the cardboard box as he retrieved it from under the bench. With Judith on her way, an itinerant approaching him in a secluded area, and the whip of sudden wind that carried with it a cool moisture that meant rain was on the way...

"No hurry, fella'. Just want to sit down, rest me legs." The man was already to the bench, and he sank down onto the end of it with a long sigh of relief.

"Good morning, sir," Clement mumbled.

The man turned to look Clement squarely in the eye, giving Clement a close view of his large, dark eyes. "Good morning to you. You been here all night, then?"

"Uh, well, on accident. I guess."

"Lucky stiff. I never get away with it." The man looked up toward the sky, and Clement followed his gaze. In the west, a deep, steely gray was building and the clouds in front of it mounted from dark to bright above them. The distant gray rumbled. Maybe Judith wouldn't even come. What was he going to do, anyhow? Go into work covered in dew, in yesterday's clothes, smelling of morning breath and night sweats? He returned to reorganizing the contents of his box so that he could close the top.

"So, tell me something about yourself."

Clement sniffed. "Why, so you can steal my identity? Murder me and cut me into pieces based on my transgressions?" He was still working at the box.

"I'm not a murderer. I promise."

"Whatever."

"Alright then, for being rude; answer my friendly question. I like stories. Who are you?"

"I'll give you the quick version before I get ahead of this storm."

"Where to?"

"That's a different question and the answer is 'I don't know.' As to the first, my name is Clement and I am an administrative assistant at an ObGyn. I lived at home with my parents—even though I'm thirty—until they died suddenly in a tragic accident. I was married to my high school sweetheart out of college, an actress. She was very successful at acting with me. I was crushed by a double blow: the wife and the economy. That same ex-wife from hell has intentions of hunting me down in this park, this morning, so I guess you understand why I need to go now, rudely or otherwise."

Clement folded the cardboard box's flaps over themselves and grabbed at his backpack just as the man also grabbed Clement's backpack. They stood there on either side of it, each holding a strap.

When Clement looked up at the man, he was shocked to see not the bearded man with the large eyes, but a darker man with a long, sallow face and no facial hair. Clement jumped back so that he was standing in a sort of crouch next to the bench with his hand outstretched toward the bag he had relinquished in his alarm. He stared as the man—who was still wearing the same outfit, had the same physique, although sort of straighter and seemingly taller—said with a smoother voice, "I am Essen." He said it like a proclamation. His caramel eyes kept Clement rapt to them. "You are the one, and I have a message for you." Essen held out his hand and opened the fingers slowly, where a crumpled sheet of paper sat in his palm.

"But you—" Clement pointed slightly at the man's face. "I mean, you—"

"I am two," said the commanding face. Then, as Clement watched with disbelief, the smooth, dark face slid sideways around until it disappeared back into the hoodie and another face—the bearded one—appeared from the opposite side. The mellower voice of the other Essen, with a changed demeanor of the whole body, coaxed, "Go on. Take it. It won't bite." He lifted the paper higher toward Clement's terrified face.

The Journey of Clement Fancywater is a novel about the hero's journey and being manly in the twenty-first century.

Is Clement the unlikely hero the world needs to save it from a power so insidious the Uplanders don't yet know of its approach? Will he find his way through a colorful, subterranean world to save humanity from the schemes of the Wizard Queen? Or is this all just too unlikely?

Look for it in 2015.

Did you enjoy this book? Please review it! We would love to have your review at Amazon, Goodreads, Barnes & Noble, Smashwords, Diesel, Kobo, iBookstore, Scribd, Oyster, or anywhere else you may want to post it. You can also request a copy for your local library.

Also find Devon at:

The Starving Artist Blog: www.devontrevarrowflaherty.com

on Facebook at Devon Trevarrow Flaherty (author)

on Twitter @devtflaherty

on Instagram at devontrevarrowflaherty

Her other books are:

Benevolent
The Touch (serialized online at Wattpad)

See devontrevarrowflahertybooks.com for more information, including discussion questions and interesting facts about Northwyth and *The Night of One Hundred Thieves*.

ACKNOWLEDGEMENTS

Thanks to my family. Thanks to those of you who live right there with me and those who manage me from afar. Thanks to Kevin, Windsor, and Eamon, to Mom and Eric and Lindsay and Dan and Braham and Ethan (who is writing-life therapy), Ma and Pa, and all the others.

Thanks to Shelly Dickey, who, despite feeling the pressure of the long arm of the digital age in publishing, has taken time out to help me along in my writerly dreams. For editing. For supporting. For encouraging. Etc. Etc. Etc.

Many thanks to and for my writing group for all the reading, critiquing, and talking it over with such compassion: David Ferrell, Justin Meckes (editor for Scrutiny Magazine and founder of Lit 101 in Durham), Sam Oches (editor for Scrutiny Magazine), and Matthew Talamini. You guys are a way better writing group than I had imagined, and you are all so very talented and inspirational. No matter how strangely diverse.

Thanks so much to my beta readers: Erin Crossfield, Kristina Ellis, Wendy Reece, and Hollins Williams. You all hit the nail on the head, and the story is much stronger because of your contributions.

Thanks also to my first readers and editors: Kevin and Aunt Shelly, Sam Oches and David Ferrell. Yeah, I already mentioned them, but they filled so many capacities along the way, I had to come back around.

Always last, but only because He's so important (and we know being last in a list provides emphasis): Jesus.